COFFEE, TEA,
OR MOLLY?

Other books by Cathy Liggett:

Pitter Patter

COFFEE, TEA, OR MOLLY?

•

Cathy Liggett

AVALON BOOKS
NEW YORK

Published by Thomas Bouregy & Co., Inc.
160 Madison Avenue, New York, NY 10016

Library of Congress Cataloging-in-Publication Data

Liggett, Cathy.
     Coffee, tea, or Molly? / Cathy Liggett.
        p. cm.
     Novel.
     ISBN 0-8034-9782-2 (alk. paper)
     I. Title.

     PS3612.I343C64 2006
     813'.6—dc22

                              2005037656

PRINTED IN THE UNITED STATES OF AMERICA
ON ACID-FREE PAPER
BY HADDON CRAFTSMEN, BLOOMSBURG, PENNSYLVANIA

To Michael and Kelly . . .
my pride,
my joys,
my dreams come true.

Love you!

Chapter One

"**O**ops!"

Drew Dawson felt the heated splash of tea land on his gray T-shirt at just about the same time he experienced an unexpected rush of pleasure, eyeing the pretty strawberry-blond female who had sloshed it there.

"I'm *so* sorry . . ." Her freckled nose crinkled apologetically, causing her sunglasses to slide. Greenish eyes stared at him, appearing genuinely contrite.

Caught off guard by the flash of green, he barely noticed the stream of harried travelers pushing to make their way around them. She had been shuffling in through the airport terminal door at precisely the same moment he had been exiting it. Now the two of them were clogging the middle of the threshold, frozen there by the spill.

"And it's Internationale's Green-Black blend too," she added, glaring at the styrofoam cup as if it were filled with criminal intent instead of an eye-opening brew. "It will leave a terrible stain!"

She began searching through her oversized straw purse, he assumed for a tissue of sorts. Meanwhile, he found himself doing a bit of searching of his own, perusing her face, taking in the scent of her hair. So natural so . . . familiar.

Had he met her before? But where? When? True, he'd been to Somersby, Ohio, before, but only for a quick visit in January for his brother Blake's marriage to Samantha Stevenson. This was only his second time here, and his plane had just landed. He hadn't even gotten out of the airport terminal yet where his brother would be waiting for him at the curb.

He was quite certain he'd never laid eyes on this striking woman before. Still, her face had a familiar girl-next-door look—all grown up, of course. It seemed he'd known her forever . . .

"Truly, it's not a problem," he said when she came up empty handed. "It's just an old rag." He tugged at the shirt. "Got a dozen like it. And," he bent his head to peer at the stained area on his chest, "at least it's the Internationale Green-Black blend. Has a rather distinct, robust sound to it. Not some sissy tea at all, thankfully."

He gave her the Dawson trademark grin, one side of his mouth curling up teasingly.

The sunny-looking lady laughed. "You're British?" she asked, acknowledging his accent. "You came all the way from England, and I've spilled my drink on you first thing off the plane?"

As the words tumbled out of her mouth, a blustery,

crimson-cheeked businessman blew past them, his oversized bulky suitcase nearly knocking the tea-drinking beauty over. Swiftly, Drew caught her elbow and steadied her. Then, his hand on her arm, he led her to the side of the entrance out of harm's way.

His composure regained, he shook his head and answered her question. "Actually, I just flew in from Boston. So don't fret, I won't go complaining to the British embassy about you or anything."

Again, he gave her the Dawson smile, attempting to charm her for some inexplicable reason.

It worked. Her creamy cheeks flushed pink and she stammered slightly. "It's not me exactly. It's—it's these silly sandals." She glanced at her feet. "I keep tripping in them."

Glancing down her jean skirt, it took his eyes a moment to get past her lightly tan but noticeably shapely legs . . . past her soft-looking feet with coral-polished toes . . . before settling on her shoes. Sandals that made a young woman's calves look great, but weren't so easy to walk in with their in-between-the-toe straps and high-wedged cork soles.

"Ah, yes. I know them well."

"You do?" She quirked a curious eyebrow at him.

Unfortunately for him, he did. But only because in a matter of weeks his father Edward, owner of an upscale shoe boutique in Boston, was retiring from the family business. The store had been in existence since the four Dawson brothers were toddlers. Soon Drew would have the heady responsibility of taking over the shop.

Not that it was Drew's idea. Not by a long shot. In

fact, his father began introducing the concept to him well over a year ago. Drew had been skiing with his buddies at Whistler in British Columbia when his father's first phone call came. Talk about a downhill slide. . . .

After graduating from college several years before, all Drew had wanted to do was travel and have some worldly experiences. In his heart of hearts, he had no overwhelming desire to get ensnared by the business world and family life like his three older brothers. Not that his brothers didn't lead prosperous, happy lives, but why rush things? Why work and be committed to one person when he could play, experiment, and be free?

But then his father's second call came in late spring. Drew was experiencing life as a surfer on the California coast at the time, and it was hard to give the idea much stock in that sunny place. Every morning the warm Pacific waters greeted him. Every night an awesome sunset rewarded his efforts out on the waves. Retail, inventory, and responsibility seemed unreal . . . faraway and distant.

It wasn't until his mother's pleas came via phone early that summer that he reluctantly succumbed to his parents' wishes. Judith Dawson was the one person— the only woman—he couldn't turn down.

All the while he just kept telling himself things would work out, trying to convince himself that his carefree traveling days weren't completely over. He could still manage to get away. All he had to do was find an especially competent manager to run the store while he took to the road for long weekend getaways.

"What I mean to say," he answered, without elaborating about his family's livelihood, "is that I've seen a number of women wearing those types of shoes. I've always been confounded as to how they actually walk in them."

"Not so easily, I guess." She laughed lightly as she took off her sunglasses, hanging them over the side of her purse all in one motion.

Her emerald eyes stared up at him, larger, more almond-shaped than he'd first realized. It took a great deal of effort to draw his eyes away from hers. When he finally did, his gaze landed on the turquoise raffia *M* woven onto her purse, the perfect prompt for him to say something lighthearted and inane. Something— anything—to prolong their conversation.

"So, does the *M* stand for Mary? Melody? Mountain climber? Or," he grinned jauntily, "magnificent and marvelous all wrapped into one?"

Her orbs flickered with amusement as she laughed, causing an odd, gratifying sensation to shoot through him. "How about messy?" she quipped, smiling. "With a capital *M*."

"Ah, well, so long as I didn't have to be the one to say it." He rubbed at his shirt in an exaggerated, comical way. Though inside he was feeling oddly disappointed she hadn't revealed her name to him.

Megan? Michelle? Melissa? It was hard to guess.
And why do I even care?

It's not as if he'd ever hurt for female companionship. He *was* a Dawson, after all. And trekking around the country he'd certainly had plenty of opportunities to meet his fair share of females.

"Well, again," she said most sincerely, "I'm sorry I bumped into you." Then apparently realizing how that sounded, she shook her head. Mesmerizing sun-drenched, reddish-blond locks flew in all directions. "I mean—I'm not sorry I bumped into you exactly, but you know, I'm sorry I—"

Drew held up his hand. "Really, it's fine. Truly. Don't give it another thought." Though as he watched her amble toward baggage claim, he had a sneaking suspicion he just might.

The thirty-minute ride from the airport seemed more like ten. Drew felt somewhat touched that Blake's wife Sam and their one-year-old adopted daughter, Emma, had come along for the ride too, and had welcomed him with hugs.

As was his first impression at the wedding, Blake's bride was warm and sweet, talking little about herself and her work as a director at the county's social services agency, and more about Emma and what a good dad Blake turned out to be.

Blake beamed at her compliment, raved about Emma, and then went on to talk about other subjects near and dear to his heart. By the time he pulled the family car into the driveway, Drew felt as if he and Blake had never been separated by time, distance, or life's pursuits. They were quipping at each other like they were back in grade school again.

"I hate to differ with you, big brother," Drew said, yanking his overstuffed backpack out of the trunk of the SUV, "but I wouldn't have left Boston without good reason. You definitely invited me to come to Somersby for an '*ad*-venture.'" He made a point of stressing the first syllable of the last word.

"I assumed we were going rock climbing. Cave dwelling. Or, well . . ." He glanced around curiously at the quiet tree-lined cul-de-sac where his brother's newly acquired family resided. "Who knows what strange things one might find exciting in this sleepy burg?"

Dotted with pristine Tudor-type homes and tidy trimmed lawns, the place looked as dormant as the long-haired retriever napping under the neighbor's shady oak. It bore no resemblance to the thrilling mountainscapes or oceanfronts he'd lived close to for the past few years.

Still he'd been game to give Somersby a try. At least for a week anyway. Anything in the name of new experiences. Anything to divert his mind from the loathsome fact that he'd soon be taking over his father's store.

"Ah, younger bro," his brother Blake clipped back in his own Englishman's tongue. "Always have been the hasty one, haven't you? Never quite listening to all the details."

Drew stood back as Blake closed the car trunk, his older sibling clucking all the while. It was a sound

Drew was used to, one that barely made an impression on him anymore.

However, what did register on him was the expression etched on his sister-in-law's pretty face. Standing outside the car, cuddling little Emma to her hip, she gazed at his older brother with a look of serene pride and unwavering love. A look that any man would appreciate—and hope for—from the woman he loved.

Well, you would, if you were into that sort of thing, Drew thought, hoisting his rugged backpack to his shoulder. *That kind of heavy-duty relationship*. He mentally dismissed the notion as easily as releasing his foot from one of his new Rossignol ski bindings.

"As I recall," he piped up, in no rush to let Blake off the hook so quickly, "there *were* no details. The phone conversation lasted all of five seconds, in fact. 'Adventure. Somersby. Come,' is all you said. And I thought it'd be a good idea before I—" Drew stopped himself from continuing. As far as he knew, Blake didn't know about their father's plan for Drew to take over the family's shoe boutique. And it didn't seem like his place to tell him. Their pops should do that, and he'd told Drew he planned to when the entire family got together for their traditional Cape Cod retreat over Labor Day weekend.

"Before you what?" His brother badgered in their typical Dawson way. "Before you fly off to Montana to a cowboy ranch? Or to Bermuda for deep-sea diving?"

Teeth clenched, Drew glared at his brother. "Actually, I won't be flying off anywhere for a while. Especially since I've just spent a good sum of money for you to drag me here under false pretenses."

"False pretenses?" Blake feigned a shocked look.

Drew nodded. "I know exactly what you said to me, elder *bro*," he reemphasized Blake's slang term, but with a tad of sarcasm added in. "Being the youngest and most virile of the Dawson tribe," he puffed out his chest in his stained, taut-fitting T-shirt, "I assure you I'm neither hard of hearing nor feebleminded like some people I know." He squared his eyes on his brother.

"Feebleminded?" Blake's head cocked back. "I'm barely closing in on thirty, man. Give me a break, would you?"

Drew tightened his grip on his backpack. "Just calling it like I see it." He shrugged. Turning his back on his brother, he began hiking up the front walk of Blake and Sam's new home.

"It's simply a misunderstanding, Drewster," Blake called after him.

"Mm-hmm. Oh, yes. Right." He let his facetious tone hang in the air.

His brother, Blake Thomas Dawson, Esq., never made mistakes. Not ever. Not now.

Not in business. As a skilled attorney, he'd never lost a case. And not in his personal life either, Drew acknowledged, turning to catch a glimpse of his brother as Blake grabbed Emma from Sam's arms and began to trot up the walk after him.

Nearly a year ago Blake had moved from Boston to Somersby, disenchanted with the demands of his high-pressure, high-profile partnership in a legal firm there. Typical of his karma, things worked out better than one could have ever imagined. In Somersby, Blake met Sam, the love of his life—a bright, pretty, funny lady Drew liked instantly.

But it wasn't just Sam that Blake fell for. A few days after the two of them met through Sam's Uncle Dom, a long-time friend of the Dawson family, a three-month-old baby girl was abandoned and left on Sam's doorstep. Because of Sam's position at the county's social services agency, the town sheriff permitted her to care for the infant until the parents came forward.

Enlisting Blake's legal expertise in the matter, Sam and Blake fell right in sync, caring for Emma and also for one another. By the time the biological parents gave up their legal claims to the baby, the two had become so close they couldn't imagine a life without one another, or the baby girl. They soon married and became adoptive parents to Emma Corrine. Seemingly overnight, the threesome had formed the perfect family.

Although at times Blake's actions appeared impulsive and rash, they were anything but. All of Blake's endeavors were intentional and well thought out. And they always seemed to work out fine in the end.

Though perhaps not this time, my good man, Drew thought to himself.

As he'd learned on the ride from the airport, his brother didn't have a daring, spirited feat in mind for them at all. Blake's invitation was more like a business proposition.

Blake had come up with a concept whereby he and Drew—*so nice of him to include me without even asking*—would provide all-inclusive business services for small businesses. Blake's idea was that small business owners know what they need to about the product or service they're selling, but quite often the owner isn't all that savvy about the everyday details of running a business: lease agreements, workman's comp, inventory, computer software, and so on. And generally there weren't enough hours in the day to take care of those details.

By combining their areas of expertise, Blake's legal knowledge and Drew's college degree in accounting and computer programming, the two of them could supply small businesses with that sort of knowledge.

Blake was incredibly excited about the idea. Drew could tell by how he talked nonstop all the way home from the airport. As Drew sat riding shotgun, Blake kept nudging him in the arm from time to time, telling him how good it was to see him. Then he'd steal glances in the rearview mirror as he drove, grinning openly, proudly at Sam and Emma in the back seat.

In fact, Blake was so gung ho he'd already set up an appointment for the two of them tomorrow. It was with the owner of a newly opened coffee shop—a Molly something-or-other—Drew hadn't caught the full name.

The only problem was, Drew had already made a promise to his father. Well, actually to his mom was more like it.

And seriously, Drew peeked around once more at the quiet suburban setting, *does he actually think I'd move to a no-excitement, no-thrill place like this?*

"Hey, Drew." His brother scurried behind him, Emma in his arms. "Slow down, man. Think about it now, would you please?"

There was definitely a pleading tone in his brother's voice.

Ah, well. There's a first time for everything, isn't there?

The fact brought a slight smile to Drew's face, along with a momentary feeling of vindication. How many times had his three older brothers taken advantage of his "last" place in the family lineup?

"It wasn't completely under false pretenses," Blake tried to explain. "Perhaps you heard hesitation in my voice. Maybe you heard me say come to Somersby for 'a venture' and it sounded like 'adventure.'"

"Or—or—" Drew could tell his brother was grasping at straws. "Could be that I cleared my throat while speaking and you mistook 'ahem' and 'venture' for 'adventure'."

Drew stopped stomping. Turning to level a thoughtful gaze on Blake, he offered a tart reply. "Hmm. Now that could be. Old codgers do clear their throats quite often."

Ha-ha! Touché!

Drew could tell he'd gotten to his brother with that remark. Blake's eyebrows shot up, his lips tightened into a grimace.

"Old codgers?" Blake's eyes narrowed defensively.

Under different circumstances—namely, if confronting a stranger on the street—that sort of pugnacious expression might have alarmed Drew. But it wasn't an uncommon exchange between the nearly all-male Dawson clan. In fact, it was a sort of standard with them. The brotherly foursome bantered endlessly, bickered tirelessly. But at the end of the day, they also clasped one another on the back. And they championed each other on unceasingly too.

Again Drew responded to his brother's indignation with an indifferent shrug. Turning to his sister-in-law who had pretty much been silent throughout his and Blake's exchange, he asked, "Sam, I just want to know. What do you think?"

He could tell his question caught her off guard. Her face went instantly pensive. Flipping her head back and forth between the two of them, she looked as if she were watching an intense tennis match where she wanted both contenders to come out winners.

"What do *I* think?" She bit her lip, hesitant to respond.

Drew and Blake bobbed their heads in unison. They stood awaiting her answer in silence.

"I—um—well—" she stalled, apparently gathering her thoughts.

Drew was sure Sam had known about Blake's business concept ahead of time. He was certain she and his brother were the type of couple who shared all their hopes, dreams, thoughts, as well as many precious times together.

But knowing how his brother could be—just a bit scheming at times—he didn't think she'd been privy to the ploy Blake had devised to get him to come to Somersby. Sam would have been leery of any plan that wasn't upfront, anything that could possibly put the brothers at odds with each other.

Though the fact was, nothing could pit the four brothers against each other. They all knew each other's good points, each other's faults, and that understanding was unconditional, unquestioned.

Drew knew Blake's modus operandi, how he'd plot to get his way. And frankly, Blake knew that Drew knew. They were simply razzing one another. At the moment, it seemed to be making Sam somewhat uncomfortable. But no matter. Given a little more exposure, she'd get used to their ways in no time.

"I think we should go inside," she said, finally decisive. "Yes. I'm sure you're hungry after your flight, Drew. Let's go inside and have a nice lunch and talk about this. Clear things up. You're both such intelligent, considerate, level-headed men that I'm sure the two of you can work this out."

Yes, a quick study she is, Drew chuckled to himself.

For a millisecond, her answer appeared to snuff out the sparks between him and Blake. But then, he couldn't resist ribbing his brother just a wee bit more as they turned once again and continued up the path to the front door.

"You do realize she was looking at me when she mentioned the word *intelligent*," Drew informed his older sibling.

"You? What the devil? She's my wife, man. No way was she looking at your ugly mug."

"I tell you the woman is smart. She knows who's the better between us," Drew smirked.

"Smart?" Blake rose up straight, taking Emma along for the ride. "She's not *smart*. She's brilliant. And you've got it all wrong. Just like that time you thought Susan Hatcher wanted *you* to take her to junior prom instead of me."

"Susan Hatcher always fancied me more," Drew quipped as he held out his hand for his brother's door key.

"You were only in eighth grade!"

"What can I say? She liked younger men."

"Right, right . . ." Blake mumbled, turning the leather fob over to Drew.

Unlocking the door, Drew held it open for Blake and the two beautiful females in his brother's life.

Honestly, it did feel good to be in his brother's company again. And he was looking forward to getting to know Sam and Emma even better.

But living in a place like Somersby? Settling down, working and living in a small town like this? He'd hate disappointing Blake at the end of the week.

But really. Even if he wasn't already committed to their father, surely his brother knew him better than that.

Chapter Two

The last trickle of morning customers had come through Corner Coffee Café over a half hour ago, meaning it was time for Molly to straighten up and put the tabletops and newspapers back in order.

Actually, would three customers followed by five, then two and then three more really constitute a trickle? Molly wondered.

That was only thirteen total patrons for the morning, she realized, biting her lip anxiously as she wiped over a few of the tables.

She wasn't sure if she was imagining it, but it seemed since she'd opened the café several months ago, that her business was steadily decreasing instead of rising.

Certainly she hadn't changed anything in the café that would drive customers away suddenly. There hadn't seemed to be any need to. When she first

16

opened, so many people had complimented her on the pleasant, homey atmosphere she'd created. She thought she had a winner.

Glancing around, she tried to determine if anything about the place looked different to her. But nothing did. The shop was the same as the day she'd opened, dotted with round antique tables and a handful of higher, rectangular tables mixed in. All were topped with embroidered Corner Coffee Café doilies protected by a piece of glass. And each table was adorned daily with a miniature vase of fresh flowers.

Cushioned pews and overstuffed chairs lined the walls while cream-colored ceiling fans turned lazily overhead. Several daily newspapers were always on hand, or customers could choose to linger over a shelf of books. And outside there was even a small patio with several wrought iron tables kept surprisingly cool by the shady limbs of an ancient maple tree.

The feel and look of the café was everything she had wanted it to be. And she had done it all on her own, something that was very important to her. As she explained to her friend April on more than one occasion, being the only female in her family she wanted to prove she could be just as successful as her older brothers. And at first, from the initial reaction of Somersby residents, she thought she had done just that. Till recently. . . .

She scooted onto a chair at one of the higher tables. Straightening the sugar packets in their porcelain container, her thoughts made her feel suddenly weary.

Though she'd never admit it to anyone, recently she

found herself making the tiniest wishes, usually when she was tired, or her overhead totaled far more than the cash register totals.

Well . . . for just a second she'd wish there were someone who would walk through Coffee Corner's front door and set her world right. Maybe that man from Publisher's Clearing house with a whopping big check for her. Or someone with a magic wand or some high-powered fairy dust would be handy too. Or maybe someone who—

The bell over the café door sounded. She looked up abruptly, a catch in her breathing.

Do wishes really come true?

It was a man all right. And he did have something in his hand.

However, it wasn't an oversized draft for a zillion dollars made out in her name. And it wasn't a glittering magic wand either.

What it was, was a cane. A carved cherry cane that Mr. Mulligan always carried. Mr. Mulligan, a retired fireman and widower, and her best—well, make that her *only* loyal customer.

"Open for business, lass?"

Molly was sure his blue eyes had probably wooed his fair share of women in his day. They still had a bit of a glint to them though now they shone behind a pair of silver-rimmed glasses. Slightly bent over, Mr. Mulligan lingered right inside the doorway, his cane holding him steady. A wan smile further crinkled his age-etched face.

"I'm always open for you, Mr. Mulligan." She perked up at his friendly grin.

"Almost always."

She looked at him quizzically.

"I stopped by at the end of the day yesterday, but you must have closed up shop early."

"Oh, yes," she remembered. "Things weren't busy, and I had promised my friend April I'd pick her up from the airport."

"And where are all your customers this morning? If you don't mind me asking."

Molly smiled to herself. Mr. Mulligan often asked questions she minded. And often said things that didn't need to be said. Even so, she still had a certain fondness for the old guy, and generally attributed his impertinence to his age.

She watched on as he paused, not really waiting for her answer. Rather he paused before making a concentrated effort to tread over to one of the cushioned pews to sit down. It seemed to Molly that he couldn't do two things at once, so she waited till he was situated before answering him.

"I'm thinking a lot of people may be on vacation right now," she said once he'd settled in. "End of summer and all."

It was an explanation she'd been tossing around in her head. But Mr. Mulligan didn't seem to agree.

"Doubt it." He shook his head vehemently. "The Somersby County Fair starts this Wednesday. Everyone usually sticks around for that."

"Oh, you're right. Hmm. Well, maybe a lot people don't drink coffee in August then. It's so hot and humid right now." How would she know? She was a tea drinker herself. Hot tea, iced tea, sweetened, herbal.

"Naw." He waved his hand, meaning he wasn't buying that logic either. "People drink coffee every day of the year. Where's mine, by the way?"

She'd already gotten his order together and set it down before him just like she did everyday—a just-baked blueberry muffin, fresh, ice-cold orange juice, and no coffee. In light of his high blood pressure, she didn't think the coffee was a healthy choice. But every visit he asked for it. And every visit she caved in and gave it to him. It was an ongoing, unspoken battle between them.

"Coming right up," she acquiesced once again, pouring a mugful and setting it alongside his plate.

He poked at the muffin just long enough to let the steaming, black stuff cool down a bit. Then he reached for the cup and took a mighty slurp.

As always, his lips pursed and his eyes squinted like a cowboy in a western, grimacing over a shot of saloon whiskey. Then he let out a pleased "ah."

"I know I've said it before, Molly girl, but it tastes just the way my beloved Mary Ellen used to make it. Strong. Black. One cup of her coffee in the morning, and I knew I'd be good to go all day long. All day long," he repeated. "Of course, when the blood pressure business started, she tried to get me off the stuff. But we'd been married for so long by then, I was hooked."

His forehead creased as his voice grew softer. "Mary Ellen. She was always so worried about me. Worried about my health. Worried I'd get hurt on the job. Caught up in a backdraft or something. All that worrying," he shook his head, looking totally bewildered, "and now I'm the one who's still here and she's not. Lord only knows how I miss that bride of mine."

His admission broke her heart, and she sat down on the bench directly across from him, ready to listen. She'd never seen Mr. Mulligan quite so misty-eyed, and for a moment, her problems were forgotten. Lost in what he had to say, she didn't even notice the sound of the bell as the café door opened.

But surprisingly Mr. Mulligan had. He ducked his head toward her. "Don't worry about me." He patted her knee. "Looks like you've got business, darlin.'"

Turning around, she tried to put on her best "customer" smile. But it wasn't a customer at all. It was— oh my gosh! Blake Dawson.

She'd meant to cancel their appointment. She'd made it a month or so ago, before business had turned from bad to worse and at a time when she thought his expertise would be useful.

"Hope you don't mind that I'm a bit early," Blake said with an apologetic smile. "And I hope you don't mind that I brought my brother along."

Molly barely heard his words, her eyes were too busy taking in the person next to him.

His what?

She blinked once. Then blinked again.

"It's—" she faltered, her finger pointing limply.

"You!" Blake's brother finished her sentence.

"Pardon me?" Blake sounded puzzled. Molly could sense him glancing back and forth between his brother and her. Meanwhile, she stood transfixed, her eyes taking in the younger Englishman. "Should I be getting the rather strange impression that you two know one another?" he asked.

Blake's brother seemed to be in shock, too, staring at her blankly at first. Then as the look passed, he cocked his head and let that slow, easy smile loose on her. "Not formally." He gave a slight bow in her direction.

"We, uh, we uh—" she rubbed at her neck, which felt suddenly, uncontrollably flushed and uncomfortable.

For a split second she wondered if the air conditioning had given out. But then, no, she heard it kick back on. Surprisingly, the ceiling fans were still spinning on cue too. "We bumped into each other . . . at—at the airport," she explained to Blake.

"Lit-er-al-ly," the brother said in that alluring accent of his.

He winked at her as if they'd secretly planned the whole thing, and the flushed area on her neck crept upward. She could feel it blossoming into rosy blushes on either cheek as her eyes involuntarily glanced at the scene of the accident—his chest.

The chest she'd spilled hot tea on less than twenty-four hours before.

The chest now clad in a black T-shirt that looked invitingly fit and overtly virile, especially next to Blake in his blue oxford cloth shirt and striped tie.

She also blushed because admittedly she'd thought about the mystery man behind that muscular physique several times the evening before. Especially after she'd dropped April off with her husband Ryan. Ryan had also just returned from a business trip and pulled into the driveway right after she and April had. The young newlyweds greeted each other so sweetly and passionately that any observer would've thought they'd been apart for decades instead of a long weekend.

And for just a moment, Molly wished . . .

Well, it seemed she'd been making a lot of wishes lately, hadn't she?

"So the *M* stands for Molly then?" The brother's warm brown eyes caught and held hers.

"The *M*," Blake spoke up. "What *M*?"

"Katz," she had the presence of mind to say.

"Drew." He extended his hand.

She slid her hand into the solid fold of his. His handshake gave her a warm and secure feeling. She was thankful when Mr. Mulligan piped up from his seat, prompting their clasp to break apart.

"Well, now that you're all acquainted . . . I'm Aidan Mulligan, and I'm the one you'll have to answer to if you're not good to my Molly here. She's a nice young lady, and bakes the best blueberry muffins you've ever tasted."

The old man didn't look like much of a threat as he worked to rise to his feet, using the cane to hoist himself up. When his effort looked a bit shaky, Drew edged himself closer to Mr. Mulligan, presumably to rescue him if necessary. Strong and athletic-looking, Drew appeared as if he could easily carry the elderly ex-firefighter over his shoulder all day long.

Meanwhile, Molly went behind the counter to prepare a sack of muffins. Baked fresh that morning, the goody bag was part of her routine with Mr. Mulligan.

"Hope the guys at the firehouse like them." She handed them over, knowing the fire station was always the next stop on Mr. Mulligan's agenda. "I tried something a little different today with the cranberry nut."

"They don't mind me pokin' around the firehouse as much when I have these." Mr. Mulligan beamed, holding up the sack in his free hand.

"I'm certain they enjoy your company with or without my muffins," Molly assured him.

Mr. Mulligan's eyes were still twinkling at her compliment when Drew helped him out the door. Then Drew and his brother settled into the plaid cushioned stools in front of the counter.

"What would you like?" She leaned over, her arms resting on the counter's edge.

It seemed like an innocent enough question. But when she looked from Blake to Drew, the younger brother's eyes were contemplative yet playful, studying her in a way that suggested he might be considering more than what her café had to offer.

Oh, of all mornings to be wearing this messy pony-tail! And why couldn't I have taken one second—one silly second—to dab on some lipstick?

Self-consciously patting strands of flyaway hair into place, she struggled to ignore Drew's intense gaze . . . and the tingling flush reigniting along her cheek line.

Specific. Be more specific. "Can I get either of you anything? Coffee, tea, or—"

"I'd like a cup of Earl Grey if you have it," Blake spoke up.

The sound of Blake's voice seemed to draw Drew out of his meditative state. "Have you ever tried Internationale's Green-Black blend?" He turned to his brother, clasping him on the shoulder. "I hear it has a rather bold flavor to it." He looked up at Molly then, sharing a half-cocked smile with her.

"Why, Drew, I thought you were a coffee addict," his older brother teased.

"Coffee *drinker.*"

"Whatever." Blake shrugged. "Imagine, an Englishman who doesn't drink tea." He rolled his eyes. "However," he leaned forward, confiding to Molly in a low, hushed tone, "we're not surprised actually. It's validated what our family has thought all along." He nodded his head toward his brother. "He's the adopted one."

"I heard that. And it's not true at all." Drew looked at her with such warm, plaintive puppy-dog eyes she was afraid there'd be nothing he couldn't get her to believe. "Judith and Edward—"

"Our parents," Blake chimed in.

"—had to try three times before they got the perfection they were seeking."

"Have I also mentioned," Blake edged in closer, speaking to her in a stage whisper, "that my dear younger brother has awful problems coping with reality?"

Having grown up with three older brothers herself, the Dawsons' bantering made Molly feel right at home. In fact, she was enjoying their repartee so much, she'd almost forgotten what they'd come for.

Remembering, a sinking feeling come over her as

she moved about behind the counter, preparing their two different brews. Meanwhile, Blake easily upheld the conversation.

"Drew is considering moving to Somersby to help me spearhead Business Partners Unlimited."

Plucking wedges of lemon from a bowl, she lifted her head. "Is that so?"

Somehow she managed to sound only mildly interested as she turned from Blake to Drew. Slightly nonchalant, even though thinking about the younger Englishman living in Somersby . . . with his adorable accent and soul-searching eyes . . . caused her heart to thump in overtime.

"Well, I—" Drew stammered.

"—he just needs to get a few things straightened out," Blake interrupted.

"Like—" Drew started again.

"—himself."

"Myself?"

Once again, Molly chuckled at the brotherly banter. "Sounds reasonable." She smiled.

"We appreciate you being our first client though," Blake rambled on. "We have some ideas formulated. But, of course, you're sort of our test business, so we don't expect much in the way of a fee. No fee at all to be exact."

"Well, honestly," she set Blake's teacup and miniature teapot in front of him, "I feel awful that you're here."

"You do?" Blake sat up straighter on the stool.

"And I certainly wish you hadn't flown all the way

from Boston." She turned to Drew, placing a mug of
steaming black coffee down before him.

"You don't?" Drew parroted his brother.

Is she ignorant, or what?

She'd blurted out the same sort of thing to Drew yesterday in the airport. He probably thought she was rude.
Or a ninny. Or both! He certainly had that same puzzled look as he'd had the day before.

Embarrassed, she buried her face in her hands, and
then pushed wisps of hair back from her forehead in a
dainty gesture. What she really felt like doing was to
give herself a good whack in the head.

Sliding both hands into the pockets of the chef-style
apron, protection for her pale blue sleeveless tee and
khaki skirt, she rocked back on her heels, feeling
sheepish. "Sorry. I just mean . . . my business was doing so well before and lately . . . the numbers . . .
well . . ." she shrugged, feeling more vulnerable than
she'd ever want to admit to anyone. "There are no numbers actually. No one is really showing up anymore.
You'd think I'd poisoned them or something."

Drew took a sip of his coffee and a pained look immediately crossed his face.

How nice! she thought, noting his expression. How
incredible that he could appear so sympathetic toward
her. After all, they were practically strangers!

"Have you had any feedback from anyone?" Blake
asked.

"No, not really," she glanced from one brother to the
other.

Drew took another sip and, again, there was that same pained expression.

What a sweetheart this guy is!

"Can I get you anything?" she asked him. "A muffin? A scone? *Anything?*" she repeated herself.

"No. No, thank you." Drew shook his head repetitively, his eyes downcast. "But do you, ah, do you have any sugar?" He looked up at her.

Blake shot him a quizzical look. "I thought you preferred your coffee black."

"Normally, yes. Normally I do. But today, well . . . today I thought perhaps I'd try something a bit different. Is that all right with you?" He bristled at his older brother.

"Goodness." Blake reared back on the stool. "No need to get your knickers in a knot, Drewster. Might want to consider some caffeine management though," he murmured the last part under his breath. Under his breath, but loudly enough that Drew could hear.

"My knickers would be my business, thank you very much. And as for my caffeine intake—"

Having experienced this side of brotherly love before too, Molly intervened quickly. She plopped a container of sugar packets on the counter in front of the bickering twosome. "Here you are. Anything else either of you might need?"

"Perhaps some cream?" Drew spoke up. "Or one of those flavored creamers. Do you have anything like that?"

Molly offered him a French vanilla creamer, and then stood back to watch as Drew went to work making a concoction of his own liking. She loved the aroma of coffee, but never understood why someone would want to drink the bitter stuff. Or why coffee drinkers seemed to go to so much trouble to make the stuff drinkable. At least that had been her observation of her customers. When she *had* customers . . .

She never once thought owning a place like Corner Coffee Café would be such a big deal. Make a little coffee. Brew some tea. And baked goods were a cinch for her. But evidently she had been wrong. Coffee drinkers were more puzzling than she'd ever imagined.

"I think you have a great concept," she finally spoke up. "But, unfortunately, I don't believe it's a service I'm going to be needing. At least not any time soon."

And maybe not ever. She couldn't stand to say the words out loud.

If this business failed . . .

Well, it was just lucky that her parents were retired and rarely in Somersby. If they weren't traveling the country in their RV, they were abroad visiting castles and various inns in the United Kingdom, so they weren't all that tuned into her business. But she could just imagine the grief her brothers would give her. After all, Nick had wanted to be a silent partner in the café. Austin had offered to do a lot of the construction to help her cut costs. And Brody would've willingly given her the benefit of his marketing experience.

But she didn't want her brothers' help. Refused it, in fact. She didn't care if she was the youngest and the only girl in the family; that only added fuel to her fire.

She wanted to strike out on her own just as they had. She wanted to prove she could accomplish something by herself.

Blake interrupted her thoughts while Drew was still messing with his coffee, stirring away. Bostonian coffee drinkers were a particular lot too, it seemed.

"I can't think of any competition you have close by," Blake offered, pouring some tea from the mini pot into his cup. Sipping at the tea thoughtfully he added, "And certainly none that offer the fresh, superior baked goods you do."

"Thanks." She shrugged.

"Have you tracked the business in any way? Can you tell about the time your traffic slowed down?" he inquired.

She thought for a moment. "I have a computerized inventory system. And daily store receipts."

Drew's eyes seemed to brighten at this. "Would you like for us to take a look?"

"No." She shook her head.

His eyebrows furrowed.

"I mean. It's not that simple. My computer crashed last week. I haven't been able to reboot it since."

"Ah, well. You're just in luck then," Blake told her, clasping his younger brother on the shoulder in a fond gesture. "Drew here is quite the genius when it comes to computers. He understands all about the strange things. Another reason why we're sure he's not a full-blooded Dawson."

Blake's cell phone rang just then, and taking it from

his shirt pocket, he glanced at the screen. "Ah, it's Sam. Mind if I take it?"

Both Molly and Drew shook their heads. Blake slid from the stool, phone at his ear, and moved to a more private part of the café. Suddenly Molly's buffer was gone. It was just her and the Englishman.

"Seriously, Molly Katz, I *am* quite good with computers." Drew turned to her. "Even if you don't want to go over store numbers, I may at least be able to get it started for you again."

She wasn't sure if it was his accent, or the way his dark eyes suddenly lightened with an impish twinkle, but the way he said her name was slightly unsettling. Unsettling in an exciting, alluring sort of way. As if she were hearing it for the first time in a long while . . . as if he knew more about her than time had allowed.

Flushed and nervous, she reached for a dishrag and began scrubbing at the counter where Blake's teacup sat.

"I don't know. I'm not really in a position to pay you." She swiped again and again at the already clean countertop.

"Hmm. So we would have to depend on the bartering system then. Always a bit more interesting." He smiled slow and easy, and again she was certain the air conditioning in the café had shut off.

"Hah!" It was supposed to be a knowing, coquettish little laugh. But instead, it came out brash like a barnyard animal, or as if she were choking on something.

She really had been working too much lately with little time for social encounters. If she were going to spend most of her time in the store, she really needed to court a younger crowd of males than Mr. Mulligan. Maybe Mr. M. could send a firefighter her way sometime so she could brush up on her feminine skills. Obviously, she needed to get back in the swing of things. She had no game at all these days.

"So if you are not in a position to pay me, are you in a position to escort me on an adventure?"

"Ad-adventure?" She stuttered and blinked at him, a mixed flush of panic and delight surging through her again. Most guys started with lunch. Dinner. A movie.

Adventure?

"My good brother Blake lured me to Somersby under false pretenses." He shrugged. "He invited me here for a week of adventure, but all along his objective was to try to lure me into his business *venture*. As you can see, I packed my backpack accordingly." He glanced down at his casual T-shirt and jeans, while she tried mightily to divert her eyes and not follow his gaze.

"Clever of him." She began rubbing at an invisible stain on the side of the counter.

"That he is." Drew nodded in agreement. Then he paused before adding, "So?"

"So . . ." She looked up from the pretend stain and saw him grinning at her. Waiting. She had to think fast and hard. An adventure. Right here in Somersby. Was there such a thing?

She guessed from his longish hair that he probably wasn't the corporate type, and it might follow that country club sports weren't high on his list. Not that she belonged to the one and only country club in Somersby anyway.

If she had to place a bet, the devil-may-care unshorn locks combined with his undeniably fit physique would mean that he was probably into sports or outdoor adventures that were challenging and physically demanding. But in this county . . . hmm. It just didn't exist. Maybe she could think of something challenging in a lighthearted way. Something innocent. Fun and—

Her mind lit on an idea. "So . . . yes."

"Good. It's a deal then." He smiled and slid off the stool. "Show me the way to that computer of yours."

Chapter Three

Drew had been able to pull off his cool Englishman facade in the open space of Molly's café the other morning. But when he had followed her behind the counter, past the ovens, and into her pantry closet turned mini-office, he was anything but calm and collected.

In those confining quarters, every wonderful thing he'd been observing about her in the past hour seemed inescapably close. The light, flowery scent of her skin teased him. Her fresh-faced beauty mesmerized him. And the half dozen or so freckles dotting her nose made him want to smile.

Then there was her hair. He couldn't quite keep his eyes diverted from its sunset color as she stood next to him, bent over, peering at the computer screen. Tendrils from her ponytail fell everywhere, brushing against her creamy cheek and laying in soft waves against her neck. Why did it look so marvelously captivating to him instead of just plain messy?

And now just thinking about her, thinking of being close to her once more—in just a mere matter of thirty minutes or so—made him wince. With pleasure, of course.

"Aren't you going to eat something before you leave?" Blake asked him when he stopped into his brother's kitchen to say his good-byes for the evening. "Don't want your stomach growling through your entire date."

Seeing his elder brother with a wooden spoon in his hand instead of a court brief or Palm Pilot seemed an anomaly Drew wasn't prepared for.

"I didn't know you could cook."

"Every Wednesday evening." Blake smiled proudly as if the task was equal to a special assignment for the Queen. "Sam has a late staff meeting on Wednesdays so I come home early to be with Emma and to cook dinner."

"Poor Sam!"

"That she has a late meeting?"

"No, that you're cooking." Drew's eyes went wide. "Positively frightening actually."

"Very funny."

Blake turned back around, stirring his masterpiece on the stovetop. Drew leaned in toward him to peek over his shoulder. "And what is it you're making there?"

"It's chili." Blake rolled his eyes as if Drew should know better.

"Chili?" Drew stepped back. "It's ninety degrees in the shade outside and you made chili?"

"Well, it's not ninety degrees in here. It's a pleasant seventy-two." Blake faced his brother, ready to defend himself. "And it's not just any chili. This is a very delectable recipe, the most important aspect being the stewed tomatoes mixed in with whole tomatoes. But if one can read, one can cook and have the ability to master all types of dishes," he added authoritatively.

"I see. And what did you make last Wednesday for dinner?"

"Last week? Hmm . . . last week. Uh, I believe I made . . ." He murmured something as he turned back to concentrate on the bubbling pot.

"I didn't hear that," Drew chuckled.

"Chili. I made chili."

Drew laughed heartily. "Chili, huh? And the Wednesday before that?"

"I'm thinking perhaps it was . . ." He stared into the air contemplatively. "Oh, rot. You know what it was. But chili or no chili, it's not as easy as it sounds. It can be somewhat trying attempting to prepare dinner while watching my active though adorable daughter at the same time."

Drew glanced over at Emma who was sitting on a blanket on the floor, surrounded by a variety of toys. Content at play, she cooed "Da, da, da, da," and a variety of other singsong mumblings in her sweet little voice while she emptied objects from a plastic container and placed them back inside over and over again.

"Yes. It appears terribly difficult." Drew smiled. "Such unmanageable working conditions too."

Looking around, Blake and Sam's home felt like quite the perfect sanctuary. Done in dark greens and burgundies, it was neither too feminine nor too masculine. But it was so . . . well, domestic. Unlike the living conditions Drew was accustomed to, everything matched and seemed completely orderly and in place.

"Do you ever . . ." Drew started to ask his brother. "What I mean is, is your life nowadays, well—"

"Boring?" Blake laughed. "Is that what you're trying to ask? Believe me, brother, it's anything but. We may follow somewhat the same schedule day in, day out, but every day brings something different. Emma is learning something new all the time, and it's incredible to watch. Incredible to be a part of. Your heart swells like nothing you've ever known. And Sam . . . I can't imagine a day without her, my life without her. Things are up. Things are down. But, we're together, you know?"

Though Drew could visibly see the joy in his brother's eyes, and hear the fervor in his speech, he still couldn't help himself from asking, "But don't you ever want to, say, hang out with other blokes? Get away? Do something crazy?"

"Sometimes. But not very often." Blake shrugged. "Truth is, it's just not as important as it used to be."

"I see. Right. Well, that's good," Drew said sincerely. "I'm happy for you, Blake." He looked his brother in the eye. "Sam and Emma are wonderful. Truly."

"Thanks, man." Blake gave Drew a brotherly nudge

in the shoulder. "I appreciate you saying so." There was a moment's silence before he added, "So, you're not going to mention anything to Molly tonight, are you?"

"Do you think I should?"

"Not if you want to see her again."

Involuntarily, the thought instantly created a sickly sensation in the pit of his stomach. "Yes, right."

"Are you sure her coffee is as horrid as you thought?"

Drew nodded. "Hard to believe, isn't it? Such a lovely creature making the vilest, most awful stuff you ever tasted. Though I did get to thinking . . ."

Blake inclined his head to hear more.

"Perhaps it was just an off day. Perhaps her coffee isn't always that bloody terrible. Maybe you could stop in the café tomorrow and—"

"I don't drink coffee, remember? It all tastes vile to me."

"Yes, right. Well then, I'll stop by again. In fact, I may make a visit to the bakery I spied right in Somersby Square and do a taste comparison. Even though the shops are in different parts of town, it may help."

"Good thinking, man," Blake nodded approvingly. "Quite scientific."

Having settled that dilemma, Drew let out a breath. "Well, I suppose I'm off."

He held out his hand and Blake knew it was for the car keys. Retrieving the keys from a hook on the wall, Blake handed them to his younger brother. "You're not eating any chili then? There's plenty."

Drew shook his head as he made a path to the front door, Blake trailing after him like a mother hen. "Save it for next Wednesday. Or the one after that . . ."

"Good night, Drewster." Blake gave him a gentle shove out the front door. "Try not to wake Em when you come in."

"This is actually quite exciting," Drew told her in that ever-polite British way of his.

His face was set in a serious expression, but Molly knew he was teasing and being facetious as they stood side by side at the fenced-in corral. Gazing at the best selection of pigs that the Somersby County Fair had to offer, he added in mock sincerity, "I don't know when I've ever been in such close proximity to this vast a collection of fine, prize-winning swine."

A small squealer poked his wet snout through an opening in the metal fence just then, nudging it annoyingly against Drew's leg. "Although at the moment I'm thinking it may be a bit *too* close actually."

He backed up from the fence, wiping at his jean leg. Contorting his attractive, angular face into an exaggerated, disgusted scowl, Molly had to laugh.

"Sorry," she apologized with more of an amused smile than a sincere one. "But you did say you were looking for adventure. In Somersby, Ohio, the county fair is as exciting as it gets. Lucky for you, you came to town this week. It's something you wouldn't want to have missed, I'm sure." She batted her eyelashes at him in an overstated way, letting him know she wasn't serious.

His mouth began to quirk with humor, but then he took her cue and played along. "Goodness, no. Positively not." He struck a thoughtful pose, arm across chest, chin in hand. "Quite a venturesome experience this county fair business. I'm looking forward to viewing the blue-ribbon heifers too. Won't be sleeping a wink tonight if I miss those."

She laughed again, relieved at his good-natured response to all of the "county fair business." She had been so nervous getting ready for the evening, changing from white sailor-style capris to a short denim skirt to a pair of khaki shorts and back to the capris again. Then after abandoning those choices, she finally decided on an airy, mid-calf sleeveless summer dress printed with miniature pink and yellow flowers.

Still . . . even though she looked cool and skirt-flowing carefree on the outside, on the inside her stomach was churning. Maybe taking the Brit to the Somersby County Fair wasn't such a good idea after all. Doubts nagged at her all the while she was getting dressed and blow-drying her hair. She was second guessing her decision even more when they arrived at the fair in his brother's shiny black BMW and pulled onto the designated grassy lot, parking between two slightly dented, dust-covered pickup trucks.

But so far, so good, she thought, glancing at him.

The fair had given them something to laugh about, tease about, and plenty to look at with the odd variety of events and people. But it only worked because of his relaxing, good humor.

"There's also a bull," she told him, grinning openly.

"A bull, huh? Just one bull in this plethora of beefy, porky, drooling, grunting creatures?"

At the mere mention of drippy things, another slobbery snout shot out of the corral. Though Blake's legs were already out of reach, he jumped back even farther.

She giggled at his reflexes . . . all the while very much aware of her own. Her heart was fluttering as fast as a hummingbird's wings, making her strain to make her voice sound even and unaffected. Meanwhile, her body had turned traitorous, seeming to have developed a sudden magnetic pull toward his. For a while she tried to fight it, leaning away, till she nearly tripped over backward in those strappy, unstable sandals of hers. And her smile! Could it just, for dignity's sake, simmer down to a contained, all-knowing grin?

But then, reflexes were those involuntary things, right? And she just . . . couldn't . . . help it.

He looked—and acted—too totally adorable. He'd come to her townhouse to pick her up in a white oxford shirt rolled up at the sleeves, casually tucked into a pair of faded blue jeans, Birkenstock sandals on his feet. Simple, but deadly, the shirt accentuated his tan as much as the jeans outlined a few of the visible benefits of his obvious love for exercise.

But now with the prevailing heat, wisps of fairground dust lit everywhere, taking the sheen right out of his white shirt. His brows were arched in beads of perspiration. And a trickle of sweat snuck out from behind a lock of hair, slipping down his carved jaw line.

Yet he seemed completely unfettered by the situation. While something about his persona hinted he was a more worldly, daredevil type than Somersby was accustomed to, he still managed to fit into the provincial low-key surroundings. And though it was probably the last place on earth he wanted to be, no one would've ever guessed it. Despite the grunting pigs, unrelenting heat, unpleasant odors and madcap flyaway dust, he was still witty, still smiling, ever the consummate good sport.

Making him even more . . . attractive.

"Yes," she answered him. "Just one. Very. Strong. Bull. All you have to do is follow me," she purred.

Oh, my gosh! Had she actually purred at him? Talk about involuntary reflexes. She was so flirting with him. Face tilted upward. Body pitched forward. Lips moving slowly.

She would've felt more ashamed if she wasn't so embarrassed. Her hand flew to her face. And while it might have appeared she was shielding her eyes from the orange-pink glow of the evening sky, she was actually hiding her burning cheeks, which were as fiery red as the nose on the clown that had just passed them.

But her hand-turned-visor was no protection against his eyes, his gaze more penetrating than any setting summer sun.

"I'm all yours," he replied, emphasizing the point with outstretched hands and that irresistible British accent of his. "Just lead. I'll follow."

Molly wasn't even going to pursue the thought that he may have meant that more than one way. Especially not when her face was still burning, and not when it was still a steamy eighty-three degrees outside.

He gave a slight bow to usher her in front of him, and she gladly swooped into the flow of the crowd.

As they sifted their way through the layers of people, Molly could feel his hand on the small of her back, guiding her like the lead in a dance. A light touch that definitely tuned in her senses, she wondered that it didn't feel too possessive. Too overbearing. And all too soon.

But it didn't somehow. On the contrary, the weightless feel of his hand felt surprisingly just enough, just right. Caring but polite, allowing her to recover from her flirting escapade. She began to relax again.

"We're almost there." She looked over her shoulder at him as the crowd shuffled them along the dirt path, everyone's scuffling feet stoking up wisps of dust. He nodded, smiling at her easily as if they were enjoying a walk on a lovely Tahitian beach at sunset.

Another trickle of perspiration slid down his face, but still he grinned agreeably. She winced inwardly, touched by his obliging willingness in spite of the conditions. He really is sweet, she mewed to herself. And then she bit her lip—hard—afraid she might make that purring sound out loud again.

"Look out!"

His voice shattered her delicious thoughts. But the feel of him brought them back into focus again as he wrapped his hands around her waist and pulled her back against him. He held her in the safe nook of his chest while at least half a dozen teenaged boys about the size of small cattle stampeded their way through the crowd right in front of her.

"Are you o—?" he started to say over the din of cacophonous music and the voice on the loudspeaker announcing the tractor pull competition on Saturday. But then another heedless herd of young snorting males, apparently in pursuit of the rest of the pack, charged across their path. Drew pulled her back into his embrace again. And though she felt like a rag doll flip-flopping back and forth in his arms—a rag doll that had died and gone to heaven, of course—she stayed tight till the onslaught had passed.

"Are you okay?" he asked again.

Snuggled up against him she wasn't going to say anything as clichéd as "I am now." But it didn't mean she wasn't thinking it.

"Yes, thanks. I'm fine. Guess they let the buffalo loose in this place."

He chuckled. "Thank God that bull's still corralled in somewhere. Are we getting close?"

She nodded ahead of them. "He's at the same place every year."

He released her, and it took a few minutes for her breathing to become normal again. By that time she had led them to their destination, a clearing in a roped off section of field.

On the left side of the grassy reprieve, there sat a half dozen or so picnic tables topped with traditional red-and-white checkered tablecloths. Groups of diners lined the picnic benches enjoying hearty platefuls of barbecue ribs hot off a matching pair of industrial-sized grills nearby. Little kids ran around the tables giggling and chasing each other, faces smeared with messy, red sauce.

And on the right side of the clearing . . .

Drew laughed. "It's a *mechanical* bull? You're kidding me? This is excellent!"

While a grilled barbecue aroma sifted around their heads, she explained, "The Gregson family has the most popular barbecue rib restaurant in the county. Several of them, in fact. And they all have a mechanical bull at each of their restaurants."

But Drew wasn't listening all that closely. He was already bolting toward the bull, digging into his jean pockets for dollar bills.

Chapter Four

"**D**rew, seriously! Wait!" Molly nervously sprinted after him, the folds of her cotton dress sticking to her legs. "It's not as easy as it looks," she warned.

What if he gets thrown off? Gets really hurt? Breaks his collarbone? Or an arm? She'd feel awful. In fact, she already felt awful. Her stomach churned as she watched him pay one of the Simms boys his dollar.

"*Nothin's* as easy as it looks, little lady," he answered jauntily, in a strange mix of his English accent and a fake western one. He donned the cowboy hat the Simms boy offered, and cocked it on his head sideways. "But as long as I know you'll be waitin' for me after I manhandle this thing, I reckon that's all that matters."

Molly would've been more amused if she wasn't so apprehensive.

"Well . . . yeah . . . sure." She gave him a hesitant smile, and for an instant thought how intriguingly handsome and rugged he looked with his long hair hanging out from under the beige suede hat. "I'll be waiting for you."

Waiting to pick up the pieces! she mused.

Sure the Englishman looked strong and fit, and altogether athletic. But he was still a born and bred city boy, after all. And she wasn't sure just what type of physical activity he was used to. Plus, the Gregsons' mechanical bulls weren't exactly the tame type. They had a reputation for being as rough riding as the real thing.

She looked on pensively as he mounted the bull and settled into position. He appeared far too relaxed for his own good.

"Drew, hold on to the saddle horn."

"What?" he called from atop the mechanical beast.

"Hold on to the horn!" She pointed with her hand.

But her warning came too late. The machine started and his body flailed and flopped every which way. Meanwhile, she held her breath in dire anticipation, expecting him to go flying off into the stratosphere at any given moment. Luckily his thighs must've been strong enough to keep him holding on, locked to the bull's flanks. *Very strong and very muscular,* she surmised, blushing at the thought.

Finally he managed to lean forward and reach for the saddle horn with one hand. Obviously, he was still trying to act the part of a western stud, waving his other hand freely in the air, like something he'd seen on cable TV.

But when the bull gave a mighty buck and he slid

sideways, his left thigh nearly touching the platform, he must have reassessed the situation. Struggling, it took him a while before he could right himself. Then he grabbed for the horn, holding on with both hands for dear life.

Molly let go a sigh of relief, but her calm was short-lived. Back in the saddle again, Drew whipped off his hat and began flapping it in the air, whooping like a regular rodeo rider.

Truly, she couldn't have been happier when the bull came to a standstill, and he slid off the machine, looking quite pleased with himself. Planting the cowboy hat back on his head like he'd been born with the thing there, he ambled toward her, his legs slightly bowed after his ride.

"That was awesome!" His eyes shone with excitement. "Great fun!"

His smile was so uncontained, she felt pleased she could provide him with a few minutes of entertainment in quiet, nothing-ever-happens Somersby, even if it had jangled her nerves just a bit.

"It looked like you were having fun," she agreed. "I might even give it a ride myself if I weren't wearing this silly dress."

"Oh, no." He shook his head. "The dress is definitely not bull-riding attire. You'd have to ride the thing sidesaddle. That'd be way too extreme for that beast."

Sidesaddle? Too extreme?

It wasn't as if he was daring her, she knew. But call it an instant reaction, a knee-jerk response from her days growing up with her thrill-seeking brothers.

She'd always tried to keep up with her older siblings, toe-to-toe with them, and even one up on them whenever she could manage to. So even if Drew didn't mean to dare her, the idea—the challenge—was suddenly too tempting to resist.

Plucking the cowboy hat off Drew's head, she placed it squarely on her own.

"Got a dollar I can borrow, cowboy?" she drawled sweetly, holding her palm out, tilting her head up at him. "Just till we get back to the car?"

"Molly, really," Drew protested, looking completely alarmed. "I don't think you want to try it right now. The thing's a beast. Riding sidesaddle is crazy. Wait till you're properly dressed."

"So you don't have a dollar I can borrow?" She pleaded with her eyes, and added a flutter to her lashes.

"Well, of course, I have a dollar."

She held out her palm again, and stood waiting with her other hand on her hip. Drew fished in his jeans' pocket for a dollar bill but didn't look too happy about it, his brow creasing with concern.

"I just don't want you to get hurt, Molly," he said, holding the dollar bill in his fisted hand.

"Don't worry. I won't get hurt."

"We can come back some other time. You don't have to do this now, you know."

"Oh, I know I don't *have* to. I want to." She tugged the dollar bill from his clutch. "Thanks. I'll be right back, cowboy."

"I'll be here." His eyes looked concerned. "I'm not moving an inch."

She lowered the hat on her head and strode over to the bull, feeling Drew's eyes on her. Boy, if she messed this up after such a display of bravado, she was going to feel like one embarrassed cowgirl, all right.

But as she mounted the bull and got situated, she smoothed down her dress, took hold of the saddle horn with one hand, and held the hat high in the air with her other hand, a calmness came over her.

Just go with the bull, she reminded herself. *Don't fight it,* she chanted to herself as the machine started up.

She swayed. She rocked. She jerked. She jostled. But she held on tight, her body moving as if it were one with the mechanical beast. And before she knew it, the jarring stopped. The bull was still. The ride had come to an end.

She slid down from the machine as daintily as she could, smoothing down her dress once more. Yes, she felt pleased with her performance, but it was nothing compared to the exuberance Drew must have been feeling. Running over to her, he picked her up and swirled her around, so proud of her he looked as if he would burst.

"That was incredible, Molly! Incredible! I mean, you rocked with that bull. It jerked and tossed. But you moved with it every time."

She looked down at him, and the admiration in his eyes . . . the feel of his arms around her . . . made her heart melt and her pulse race all at the same time.

"Oh, it was nothing." She felt suddenly shy.

"Are you kidding?" he exclaimed. "You were amaz-

ing! I should hustle you out west. I could be your manager. We could make a fortune in the rodeo business."

She laughed. "Well, I'm sure the real thing is quite
different than one of Gregsons' mechanical bulls."

"Yes, but—" he sputtered, seeming beside himself
with excitement. "Sitting sidesaddle, hat flying in the
air—you were beautiful!"

"Actually, Molly," he said more softly, as he slowly
lowered her to the ground, her body grazing his till the
earth met her feet. "You *are* beautiful. Truly," he added,
gazing into her eyes, his arms still wrapped around her.

"Well, uh . . . thanks," she told him, not too sure of
what to say. But sure that she liked the feel of his embrace.

"We should go celebrate your first time, don't you
think?"

First time?

"Oh, it's not my first time. I've, uh, I've—you know,
done it once or twice," she fibbed. But only because she
hated to ruin it for him! His eyes were positively
gleaming with adoration; his enthusiasm seemed
boundless; his mood, off the scales.

And, okay, maybe she'd neglected to tell the whole
truth a tiny bit for herself too. After all, she could feel
herself glowing from head to toe in the beam of his
admiration.

Did he really need to know she'd ridden the bull *once
or twice a week* ever since she was about eight years
old, when her family would make their Friday night
trek to Gregsons' restaurant for dinner? Or how she'd

tag along with her brothers to the fair each summer, and they'd ride *once or twice a day?*

A girl was allowed to have a secret or two. Wasn't she?

"I'm not sure if neon blue, raspberry-flavored Smurf ice cream is quite the best way to celebrate your extraordinary feat, Miss Rodeo Queen. But I will say the view right here is most spectacular."

Drew was sitting next to her on a weathered wooden bench that someone at sometime had randomly placed along the riverbank of the Little Miami River. The narrow river lay at the farthest edge of the fairgrounds, completely isolated from all people and events.

But even in the dimming, forgiving dusk light, Molly knew there was nothing picturesque about the view there. The summer had been so dry and hot that the stream of water had pretty much dried up. Needless to say, all the grasses and shrubs along the riverbank were parched and brown too. Not a pretty sight!

But she also knew Drew wasn't exactly looking over her head or around it to peak at the river scenery. He was looking directly at her as he said those words. Gazing straight at her . . . causing her to let out an involuntary giggle.

"What?" he asked her, his mouth crinkling at the edge. "What's so funny?"

Oh, gosh, had she really giggled like a young, giddy school girl? How embarrassing! Good thing she had pulled off the rodeo stunt with such magnificent ease. At the moment he was holding her in such high esteem it didn't seem like anything—even a goofy-sounding giggle—could diminish her worth in his eyes.

"I don't know . . ." She felt the heat rising in her cheeks. "You just sounded so, you know . . . so British . . . and so—so flirty."

Oh! she groaned to herself. *Do I always have to utter my every last thought?*

"Well, I am British." He smiled, his voice sounding calm and even. "And I *am* trying to flirt with you."

He leveled his twinkling chestnut eyes on her, and she worked hard to squelch the uncontrollable grin that wanted to dance—make that leap—across her lips.

But then he seemed to remember the cone in his hand, and turned his attention back to his ice cream, which was melting more with each second. Taking several quick licks, he worked to get the trickling cone under control. Once he'd gotten the upper hand on it, he glanced up at her, smiling satisfactorily. A streak of ice cream topped one side of his lip, making a blue half-mustache. She giggled again.

"What now?"

"There's um, you know . . ." She nodded.

"No, I don't know."

The combination of a manly shadow across his lip and a boyish blue streak of ice cream made him look so adorable, Molly didn't know which was melting faster, her heart or their cones.

"There's ice cream . . ." She told him, pointing to the left side of her mouth.

"Here?" He immediately pointed to the opposite side of his mouth.

"No, it's—" She reached out to wipe at the spot with her fingertip, feeling his eyes gazing at her, "—right here," she told him, totally aware of the way his skin felt beneath her touch and completely conscious of the heated current flowing between them.

"Thanks," he said.

"Sure."

They both sat quietly for a moment, and Molly absently wondered when the temperature was ever going to cool off. Looking up at the sky, she saw a hint of the evening's first stars. Staring at them made her think, as they often did, of things far away . . . far away and unlike Somersby.

"Do you like living in Boston?"

"Boston?" Drew appeared surprised by her question. "Actually, I flew in from Boston. But I really haven't spent much time there since I graduated from high school, I'm afraid. I attended college at UCLA, and from there, well . . ." He hesitated and looked away for a moment as if considering his words.

"The thing is . . . for the past several years, I've been performing a series of odd jobs here and there. But that's only because my main goal has been traveling and exploring. It seems like the only time in life I'll get the opportunity, if you know what I mean."

He looked at Molly, and she nodded. Yes, she did know what he meant, but she couldn't fathom such a situation for herself. It just wasn't the way her family did things . . . not the way she'd been brought up.

"I did a lot of surfing up and down the Pacific coast," Drew continued. "But skiing is my first love. So I've skied pretty much all around the West and Northwest. Places like Whistler, British Columbia, and others of that nature."

"You're kidding!" Molly felt her eyes light up. "I love skiing. I snowboard."

"Are you serious?" His eyes gleamed with more appreciation than one incredible looking man should be allowed to bestow on any one female at any one time.

"But I've never made it to B.C." She shook her head. "I always wanted to, though. But there didn't seem to be the time. After college, I worked in one restaurant after another until I got the hang of the business. Well, I thought I had the hang of the business . . ." she murmured, realizing she was half-talking to, half-questioning herself. "Then I—I took what money I had saved and signed for a small business loan so I could afford to open the café."

"It's impressive, Molly. It really is. I mean, most people only dream about doing something as grand as you have. Few really dare to do it," he said quietly supportive. "It's quite a lot to take on by yourself."

"Well . . ." She shrugged. "There's no other way I'd want to do it. I really don't want someone telling me how to run things, you know? If I'm going to make mistakes, they'll be my mistakes. Then, if something goes wrong, I only have myself to blame. And if something goes right . . ."

Like the way things had been going in the beginning when the café had been doing so well. But now . . .

Well, she didn't want to think about all that right now. Drew seemed to be able to read her thoughts and quickly changed the subject back to a more pleasant topic.

"Do you do any freestyle riding?" he asked.

"Sometimes." She nodded. "Do you?"

"Actually last winter I spent a great deal of time working on flips, crazy as it sounds."

"Crazy? I'd love to see you do it sometime," she blurted out excitedly without thinking.

"What about you?" he asked.

"Oh, well, I don't get to ski as often as I like. And the season around here is fairly short. But I've managed to master some aerial rotations."

"Not too shabby," he commended her. "I'm quite impressed."

They grinned at each other openly and Molly knew that even if they hadn't shared a day of skiing together, their passion for the slopes was enough for them to bond.

"It really is the best, isn't it?" She sighed.

"Incredible." He nodded. "When you land a jump, it's like some aerodynamic ballet. An incomparable feeling!"

"Or taking the first run in the morning," she spoke softly, recalling past ski experiences. "When everything's quiet . . ."

". . . the snow's untouched. Unscathed. And you can set down virgin tracks," he finished her thought.

"It's awesome," she said in quiet agreement. "So awesome."

Suddenly she felt the ice cream dripping onto her fingers. She'd been so busy gabbing and reminiscing she'd forgotten it was in her hand. Hurriedly, she slurped at the melting ice cream, circling it with her tongue till she contained the dripping blue liquid.

Looking up at Drew, she smiled.

He took one look at her and laughed.

"What?" She scrunched her eyebrows at him.

"Ice cream."

"Huh?"

"You've got ice cream on your lips."

"Oh. Here?" She dabbed at the left corner of her mouth.

"Not quite." He shook his head, grinning.

"Here?" She dabbed at the right corner.

"Uh-uh." He laughed.

"Well, where then?" she asked, exasperated.

"Right here," he said, shifting to face her.

She steeled herself for the feel of him . . . for the touch of his fingertip lightly brushing across her mouth. But what she hadn't been prepared for was the feel of his lips as he lowered his mouth to meet hers in a soft, shivery kiss.

Breathless. That's how she felt when he pulled his lips apart from hers. Not the kind of breathless when you're frightened, or shocked, or unsure, but a wispy, wonderful kind of breathless. A can't-believe-it's-true sort of breathless.

They sat on the bench in silence for a moment. She, for once, couldn't think of what to say. But she noticed Drew looked suddenly pensive, contemplative, as if he had a lot on his mind.

"What are you thinking?" She braved herself into

asking him. Was he sorry that he'd kissed her? Did he think *she* was sorry that he'd kissed her? Because she wasn't. Even though in terms of days, hours, and minutes, they hadn't spent much time together. In terms of closeness, it seemed to her as if they had.

"Pardon?" he answered, looking right at her though his eyes appeared distant. His lips formed a tight, forced grin. "Oh, nothing, really." He shrugged his squared shoulders. "Why? Do I seem buggered by something?"

She nodded.

"Really? Well, I'm not. It's been a wonderful evening, Miss Molly Katz. An incredible, unexpectedly delightful evening here in Somersby."

But she could tell he wasn't being completely honest. He was definitely thinking about something else. And as much as she wanted to press him and know what was truly on his mind, she didn't. She guessed a man was allowed to have a secret or two sometimes. At least until she pried it out of him. . . .

Chapter Five

"Drew?"

He swung around at the sound of Molly's voice, hot coffee sloshing out of his Perk Up coffee shop to-go cup. He'd stopped there to do a taste comparison test just like he'd mentioned to Blake the night before. And now he'd been caught red-handed. He winced at the thought, and at the painful sensation of the spilled steaming brew on his skin.

"You're out early." She smiled up at him, seeming not to notice the coffee cup—yet.

The sun was already beating down on the sidewalk that lined the periphery of Somersby Square. Most businesspeople had made their way to their designated offices and shops, but a few others who presumably had the day off lingered on the square. One older couple sat staring out into the day on a white painted bench flanked by pots of red geraniums. A few early-bird moms had gotten their crews dressed and were pushing baby carriages or tugging at smaller children behind them.

Squinting into the sun at Molly, he found himself stammering. "Yes, yes. Right. Out early today."

He tried to hold his newspaper in the same hand as the coffee, hoping to hide the cup behind it. He could feel the crook of his thumb burning as more coffee splashed out onto his skin.

In a strange way, he felt like he deserved it. He felt terrible for purchasing the coffee from some place other than Molly's. But even worse than that—he felt completely traitorous for enjoying it so much. It was the best cup of coffee he'd had in days, particularly since he'd arrived in Somersby.

Not that Perk Up was in direct competition with Corner Coffee Café by any means. Somersby Square, right in the center of town, was a world unto itself. Whereas Molly's café was out in the suburbs and had plenty of traffic of its own to attract.

His whole point had been to try some other Midwestern coffee just to make sure it was comparable to the coffee served up East. In the case of Perk Up it wasn't only comparable, it was superior. And he felt bloody awful for thinking so. Not only that, he felt totally remorseful for thinking so poorly of Molly's coffee. Plus, incredibly guilty that his desire for strong black java had been satiated by another woman.

"You're looking quite cute this morning," he told her not only because she did but also because he was making every effort to distract her.

"You think so?" She cocked her pretty pixie face sideways.

"Yes. Great shade of lipstick. And I'm thinking . . . did you do something different with your hair?"

She laughed off his compliments, and shook her head at him. "Okay, fess up, Drew Dawson. What are you trying to hide?"

"Me? Why would you say that? What would I have to hide?"

"I don't know," She peered at him with an amused, but curious look on her face. "Just a feeling . . . just a guess."

How did she do that? It was uncanny actually. He'd never felt so transparent with anyone else before in his life. She seemed to see right through everything he did. She knew when he was using his British charm to woo her. Knew when he was hiding something. Knew when he was thinking something. Just like last night . . .

After he'd kissed her, he sat back studying her face and had the most unsettling, peculiar thoughts. Somehow he actually found himself thinking how lucky he was to be with her at the Somersby County fairgrounds of all places, instead of on the beach with his surfing buddies. Quite a disturbing, bewildering thought indeed. Who knew where on earth that kind of notion had come from?

"Uh, Drew." Her voice brought him out of his reverie. "Your newspaper is dripping."

"What? My newspaper?" He glanced down at his hand, at the sloppy mess, and shook his head. "It's confounding how I do things sometimes. I had everything in my left hand so I could, um," he tried to cover up quickly, "yes, so I could shake hands with, um . . ."

"Walter?" Molly chirped up.

"Walter?"

"The man who owns the newspaper stand?"

"Oh, yes, right! Walter it is. I'm so bloody dreadful with names." He grimaced at her. "Thank you for re-minding me, Misty. It is Misty, isn't it?" He winked.

He heard her laughing as he walked over and threw the dripping paper and cup of coffee in the garbage can. Disposed of it reluctantly, feeling at once relieved and sick at heart. How he'd been craving a good cup of coffee.

"So why are you out so early?" Molly asked him as he stood wiping his hands together, the scent of strong black coffee still on them, taunting him.

"Oh. I'm, uh . . ." He was trying to think of his next fabrication, when she provided it for him.

"Are you stopping at Chaussures to visit Dominic Barnaclo? I heard he's a friend of your family's. His niece Sam married your brother Blake, right?"

"Right, right." He straightened up, nodding agree-ably, feeling relieved.

"I know because Sam's the director of the children's social services agency where my friend April works."

"Imagine that!" Drew clapped his hands. "Small world, huh?"

"You have no idea." She shook her head. "Well, I left Mr. Mulligan manning the café for me while I ran an errand, so I've got to run."

"Okay, well . . ." He was trying to think whether he

should ask her to dinner or a movie or both, but there didn't seem to be time. She had hitched her purse over her shoulder and was already turning to go.

"See you later, okay?" She smiled sweetly.

"Uh, sure. Great."

He stood on the sidewalk for a moment after Molly left, feeling somewhat off kilter by his encounter with her—and her abrupt departure. Plus, there was something else nagging at him . . . he just couldn't put his finger on it.

Trying to slough off the feeling, he started over to Chaussures as Molly had suggested. But he'd only taken a few steps when he stopped dead in his tracks.

Wait a minute. He blinked down at the pavement. He had just kissed the girl less than twenty-four hours ago, hadn't he? And for most of the ladies one Dawson kiss just wasn't enough, was it? Most other girls would be lingering over their good-bye, expecting another, or making plans for the next get together, or . . .

But Molly seemed to be in a hurry to get away from him, didn't she? Was he losing his touch? Had the Dawson charm somehow diminished, seemingly overnight?

It just couldn't be.

Or could it?

It was another unsettling, altogether disturbing thought. But since last night with Molly, "disturbing" seemed to be the new theme for his visit to Somersby.

Molly did hate to run off from Drew, but she really had left Mr. Mulligan in charge of the café. Not that it would be all that challenging for her dear, elderly friend. She'd already taken care of a few early-morning patrons. So from now until closing, the café would probably only bring in another handful of customers.

But honestly, that wasn't the only reason she was trying to scurry away from the Englishman. She was also afraid if they continued to chat for too much longer he might find out why *she* was paying a visit to Somersby Square. Deftly as ever, she'd managed to keep the conversation focused on him—and off her.

She was just relieved he hadn't seen her come out of the Sterling Pavilion. He may have had some questions about that, or with his brother's help, put two and two together. No way did she want to tell him that she was only able to pay part of her café rent this month and had to meet with her landlords, Prescott Sterling IV and his irksome mother Genevieve, about some kind of payment plan. Nor did she want him to know how unreasonable they were and how close she was to losing her business.

After all, the way he'd looked at her last night—and kissed her last night—he'd seemed so proud and awed by her. And to tell him that her business was in even worse shape than he probably imagined . . . it'd be so humiliating. She just didn't have the nerve to.

She stood on the sidewalk and sighed up into the blinding sunlight. Ideas for the café and images of Drew whirled around in her head. What she needed was an April fix. Either April would be in one of her quirky, flighty moods and take Molly's mind off her problems. Or April would be in a focused mood and help her clear her mind. Either way, Molly decided, a quick dose of her best friend was just what she needed right now.

Glancing at her watch, she figured Mr. Mulligan could probably handle the café for a few minutes longer. The Children's Social Services Agency was right up the block. It would only take an extra minute or two to stop in and say hi to her friend.

She had decided to look business-like that morning, wearing black pants and a short-sleeved black knit top for her meeting with the Sterlings. But the dark-colored outfit seemed to absorb every ray of the sun, so ducking into the air-conditioned agency was a welcome reprieve.

Standing in front of April's reception desk, she squinted, adjusting her eyes to the indoor light. The desk was covered with files, papers, and a couple of framed photos, but there was definitely no April in sight.

Figuring her friend was probably in the restroom, Molly took a few seconds to bend over the desk, getting a closer look at the photos there. The one of April and Ryan on their honeymoon was definitely the best and brought back memories of how excited they'd been when Molly got them a discount through her aunt's agency for their dream-come-true trip. Hugging each other with a Caribbean beach as their backdrop, the two of them looked tan, content, and totally in love.

As she picked up the picture of the happy couple, an image of Drew popped into her head. Drew Dawson. Not even a week ago she'd bumped into him at the airport, and suddenly he seemed to be showing up everywhere. In her café, on the streets of Somersby, in her thoughts. Not that she minded really.

She'd been wishing for someone to come into her life for a while now. Just so that someone didn't want to take over her life. Most guys, even her brothers, seemed to want to take control—to change her, save her. Didn't they know that was totally the wrong way to win her heart? She'd push them away without another thought.

But Drew was someone she felt drawn to, someone she *wanted* to get to know better. And he didn't seem like he'd ever be that way at all. Like the other day, when he'd spent the morning fixing her computer. He didn't try to act like Mr. Computer Guru, telling her she needed this equipment or that. He didn't try to change her software or her way of thinking to his. He simply cured her immediate problem without a word and got her system up and running again.

And then last night, the way he'd been so excited and swung her around in his arms . . . the way he'd kissed her . . . that didn't seem pushy either. It seemed totally natural and right.

Maybe he is the one . . .

Startled by her own thoughts, she thrust the photo of the newlyweds back into place. Glancing around the empty reception area again, she peeked at her watch, a nervous twinge plucking at her stomach. She was all out of time and needed to get back to the café. Grabbing a pen and pad from April's desk, she started scribbling a quick note to her absentee friend.

She was lost in thought when a soft voice greeted her and startled her as well. "Can I help you?"

"Oh!" She jumped. "I'm Molly. Katz. April's friend. I hope it isn't a problem. I didn't see her. Just thought I'd leave a note."

"Molly Katz?"

The smile that burst across the woman's pretty face made Molly feel instantly warm and welcome. With sunny blond hair bouncing as she walked, the woman came around the desk, leading with her outstretched hand.

"I should have known it was you. April has told me all about you and your wonderful café. And my husband's brother, Drew, has mentioned you—oh—" She rolled her eyes toward heaven as if she was searching for some high number there. "Let's just say on more than several occasions."

"You're Sam? I mean Samantha?" Molly clasped the friendly hand.

"You had it right the first time. I'm Sam. And I'm sorry, but April isn't here. She went to a seminar for United Way this morning. But I'm glad you stopped by because, well, I haven't mentioned this to Drew just yet, but Saturday evening we're grilling out. April and Ryan are coming over, and I was hoping—please tell me if I'm out of line here—but since I don't know how long Drew will be here, I was hoping you could come too."

Doesn't know how long Drew will be here?

Surely, she had heard Sam wrong? Wasn't Drew starting a business with his brother? Or did the brothers have business that would take them out of town?

She tried to hide her confusion so Sam wouldn't mistakenly think it had anything to do with the invitation she'd extended.

"I've love to, thanks. I'm not exactly sure where you live, but . . ."

"Don't worry. I'll send Drew to pick you up around seven. Does that sound okay?"

"Sounds great," she nodded, glad that she had stopped by.

Sam was just as nice as April had always said, and she could instantly see why the agency director was a perfect match for Blake Dawson. It also seemed Drew's new sister-in-law was trying to play matchmaker for him, a thought that kept Molly smiling all the way back to the café.

Chapter Six

"Isn't that your second rather large piece of Molly's pie?" Drew asked Ryan.

Like everyone else seated around the outdoor table, Molly turned her attention to Ryan, zeroing in on his dessert plate. The salad, steaks, and baked potatoes Sam and Blake served had already been devoured and cleared from the table. Round two was a freshly baked peach pie that Molly had offered to bring.

Though Drew's comment sounded harsh, Molly knew it wasn't meant to be. He was only ribbing Ryan. She could tell by the way Drew turned to April and winked.

"Can't help it, dude," Ryan confessed to Drew, pausing momentarily with his fork in midair. "This is the most awesome pie I've ever tasted. Hands down the best, Molly." Ryan glanced across the table at her.

"Thanks." She smiled back.

"But what about next weekend, chum? I thought you were going rock climbing with us." Drew continued to tease, not letting Ryan off the hook so fast.

"That's a week away. I'll work this off by then. Besides," Ryan took another bite, his words muffled slightly, "I can't resist."

"Yes, well, I can empathize." Drew looked over at Molly, his gaze settling over her. "I'm having a tough time resisting myself."

To everyone else seated at the table, Drew's comment probably sounded innocent, as if he was only talking about dessert. But Molly knew better. She could sense the double meaning of his words, could feel it in the way his eyes penetrated her, and in the way his look stirred every inch of her with an excited tremor as she sat next to him.

Luckily, the brick patio was dimly lit with only an assortment of pillar candles and some torches lining the periphery, so no one could see her flushed cheeks. Luckily, April always came to her rescue, even at times when she didn't know Molly needed rescuing.

"That's Molly, Queen of Confections," her friend piped up. "Makes the sweetest and is the sweetest."

"Mmm . . ." A slight moan escaped Sam who with closed eyes seemed to be savoring her own piece of pie at the other end of the table. "It *is* delicious, Molly."

"Isn't it great?" April chimed in again. "I'm not into coffee or tea. Never liked a hot drink. But Molly's baked goods? I'll gorge myself on them anytime."

"How did you ever learn to bake like this?" Sam asked.

Usually Molly felt shy being the focus of any compliment, but somehow sitting in the midst of this group she didn't at all. All night she'd felt comfortable, totally enjoying their easygoing conversations and light-hearted laughter.

Sam's question made her stop and think for a moment. "From my grandmother, really. I grew up with three older brothers. And generally from morning till night I tried to keep up with them, following them wherever they'd go. Except for when we went to our grandmother's house." She paused, picturing the indelible scene in her mind.

"My brothers would run around her backyard, wreaking havoc. But at those times I stayed right where I wanted to be, glued to my grandmother's side. She could bake anything from scratch—without recipes even. And that's what we'd do. I think I inherited her techniques without even realizing it."

The patio doors opened just then, and everyone turned to watch as Blake resumed his place at the table.

"Is Emma doing okay?" Sam asked him.

He shook his head. "Seems a bit fussy. But I managed to get her back to sleep. I hope she's not coming down with something."

"I've heard there's a summer flu going around," April spoke up. "Too bad she's not older. I have a great herbal preventative."

"Maybe the rest of us should be taking it," Sam answered her.

"So what did I miss?" Blake threw out the question.

"You've practically missed out on Molly's incredible peach pie," Drew told him. "There's not much more than crumbs left actually."

"That's okay. My beautiful darling wife will share a bite or two of hers with me." Blake turned to Sam. "Won't you, beautiful darling wife?"

"One bite." Sam leveled her eyes on him. "Maybe two. But no more. Sorry." She raised her brows in apology. "It's far too good."

True to her word, she cut into her slice of pie, bringing a forkful to Blake's lips. "Wow." He blinked in amazement, sampling a taste. "That is—it's incomparable. Incomparably delicious," he told Molly. "No wonder my typically generous wife didn't want to share." He winked at Molly and then smiled at Sam.

"Oh, well . . ." Sam seemed to have a change of heart, smiling lovingly back at him. "For you, I'll sacrifice. I'll give you one more bite."

She held the fork to his lips once again. It was such an intimate gesture, everyone at the table watched, spellbound. But clearly, Blake and Sam only had eyes for one another at that moment, holding one another's gaze as Blake tasted more of the pie. Then he bent closer giving her lips a sweet, delicate kiss.

The host and hostess' loving exchange seemed to set off a chain of reaction around the table. Ryan grasped for April's hand with his fork-free one, pulling their clasped hands into his lap. Drew turned to Molly with such a look of longing she couldn't help but look back at him the same way. Their gaze was broken when Blake spoke up.

"Molly, did you know we have a lake in the neighborhood?"

She shook her head, wondering how he'd segued to that particular topic. "You do?" she asked politely.

"Yes. And it's actually quite charming." He nodded. "You really should have Drew show you. He jogs around it almost everyday, don't you, Drew?" Blake asked his brother.

Drew nodded and Molly smiled. *Oh, so that's the connection.*

"It is quite nice," he told Molly. "I jog on the walking path surrounding it, about two miles around the periphery. There's even a little community rowboat docked there. For the brave of heart, I assume." He gave her a crooked grin.

"You'd like it, Molly," April chimed in. "We took a walk down there the last time Sam and Blake had us over. You really *need* to see it," she emphasized with a wink.

My, there was a lot of winking going on tonight, Molly thought. *And so many matchmakers too!*

"I wasn't sure you'd want to take a walk with me," Drew told her as they ambled down the sidewalk toward the lake.

The neighborhood was quiet and, except for the two of them, the tree-lined streets were deserted for the moment. It seemed to be the in-between time of night when the younger kids had been put to bed after a hard summer day at play. And the older kids were still out, cruising around in their cars till curfew time.

A star flickered overhead as Molly turned her face up to answer him. "Really?" She was caught totally off guard.

He nodded. "Really."

"Why? What would make you think that?"

All evening, she thought she'd been sending signals telling him otherwise. Because she, for one, couldn't wait for them to be alone. The dinner had been great, and everyone had been wonderful. And she was elated that Sam had invited her. But sitting next to Drew all night, underneath the stars, had made her wish more than once that it had been just the two of them sharing a candlelight dinner—or some alone time like they'd shared the other night.

"Well . . ." He started, and then paused. "The other day when I saw you at the square, you seemed . . . I don't know. I just hope the other night at the fair I didn't force you into something you didn't want."

"Believe me, you don't have to worry about that. I'm not easily forced into things."

"Well, I didn't think so. But, well . . ." He cocked his head at her, looking mildly relieved. "Good then. I'm glad."

Approaching the lake, they took the stone steps leading down to the walking path surrounding the lake. For a moment, they stood in silence taking in the view. Beautiful flowers and lush plants were strewn everywhere at their feet; scatterings of stars created a lacy canopy over their heads. Meanwhile reflections of moonlight danced capriciously on the water as choirs of crickets provided background music.

Drew reached for her hand while they stood there taking in the view. He folded it gently into his. "Is this okay?" he asked.

Is it okay? The moment was too perfect and he was too close not to be touching her. She'd been waiting several days—and all evening thinking about it. It was more than okay to her. She nodded and squeezed his hand back in reply.

"It's not the Thames or the Charles River," he said in a hushed voice, his accent sounding particularly pleasant.

"And thankfully not the muddy Ohio—or any of its tributaries," she added, thinking of the setting several nights before.

"But it's still worth the walk," His thumb rubbed over hers, "wouldn't you say?"

"Definitely," she said, shivering at his touch.

They'd been standing there for a while enjoying the scenery and their closeness when he asked, "So what do you think?" He nodded toward the rowboat pulled up on the bank nearest them. "Do we dare?"

"Yes." She laughed. "Of course we do!"

Making their way down to the water, they loosened the rowboat from its spot on the bank.

"Want me to help row?" she asked him when they'd settled into their places in the community boat.

"No. No. I think I can handle it." He smiled.

And he did. In a matter of minutes, with oars moving through the water at an even, easy pace, he rowed them out into the middle of the serene lake.

"Let me know if you get tired," she offered.

"Oh, not to worry. You'll be the very first to know."

Feeling relaxed just being with him, she sat back, looking out on the dreamy water. Thinking back over the past week, she sighed. The few times she'd been with Drew seemed so special . . . so perfect and effortless. How she wished she could enjoy their time with one hundred percent of her being. But with her business in jeopardy, and the uncertainty of her future, she just couldn't fully give in to her feelings. As much as she wanted to be present in this moment, the problem was always there nagging at her. She sighed again.

"Two pence for your thoughts."

She made light of his offer. "Hmm . . . double the normal rate. Watch out, I may take you up on it."

"You should, Molly."

"Oh, it's nothing." She shook her head. "Really."

He pulled the oars out of the water and drew them inside the boat. Leaning forward, looking into her eyes in that irresistible way of his, he urged her. "Come on now, Molly Katz. If we're going to get to know one another better, you need to tell me what's on your mind."

"Oh, yeah?" She leaned toward him. "When I asked you the same thing the other night, Drew Dawson, you didn't tell me what *you* were thinking."

"That's different." He smirked.

"Different how?" She straightened, smirking back.

"Because." He shrugged a shoulder and tried for a cocky tone. "I'm the male here. I'm supposed to be mysterious and self-contained. And with my English accent even more so."

"Really?" she drawled out the word, shaking her head, incredulous. "And I'm a female, so I'm supposed to blurt out whatever is on my mind?"

But he only laughed. "It doesn't seem to have stopped you before."

Knowing what he was saying was completely true, she laughed right along with him.

"You're right. I do have kind of a problem with that, don't I?"

She could see his shoulders relax, his eyes lighting on her, shining intriguingly in the moon's light. "I wouldn't say it's a problem, actually. Not at all. In fact, it's one of your endearing qualities. One of the things I lov—" He stopped short. "One of the things I like about you."

"Oh?" She sat back, preening at his admission. "And so," she ventured, feeling a bit full of herself, "when do I find out what's on your mind?"

"To be quite honest . . ." He knocked on his head, "not much up there usually. Besides, it's a tricky process. I think what happens is that somehow in your uniquely female sort of way, you help me to discover my feminine side so I'll talk easily and freely about my feelings. And of course it's all done in such a manner I don't even realize what's happening. In the end, I think I've found my inner self all on my own."

"Hmm. Interesting . . ."

"Or bloody heck with that. You could just hold me

down and kiss me, and I'll tell you anything you want to know."

She laughed off his suggestion, but the thought of doing just that made her skin tingle. She hugged her arms to her chest.

"Chilled?"

"Uh-uh. Not really." She shook her head.

"So . . ." He gave her one of his heart-stopping, lop-sided smiles. "Are you, or are you not, going to tell me?"

Feeling as if all her defenses were suddenly melting away, she hugged her arms even more tightly around herself. "I don't know. It's just . . . it's been so good with you this week. I can't believe I bumped into you. You were just a stranger in the airport. And then all of this. It's been so great, and I'm so happy I met you. But then—"

She paused, hating to go on, but Drew was looking at her expectantly.

"But then, what?"

"It's awful too."

"Awful?" A sick look crossed his face.

"Not awful as in *awful*. It just seems to emphasize the sorry state of the café. I wish so badly I could just enjoy being with you without all that other worry dragging me down."

"Yes, well, it would be nice if life were neat and tidy in that respect."

"Definitely." She nodded, uncrossing her arms. Pushing against the boat's wooden seat with her hands, she willed herself to go on. "But I think . . . I think tonight has made things a little clearer for me," she confided. "I'm pretty sure I know what the café's main problem is."

"You do?" He sat up completely straight, looking at her intently. "You know?"

It was adorable how he seemed to be holding his breath, hanging on to her every word. His concern made her feel even more confident.

"Uh-huh." She nodded. "The problem is—my baked goods."

"Excuse me?" He drew back, his brows furrowed.

"I think I should have more of them. I should make my baked goods the focus."

"But the name of your establishment is Corner *Coffee* Café," he stressed.

"Oh, I know." She shrugged. "But it's just a name. And, I mean, I'm not boasting or anything, but Mr. Mulligan acts like the guys at the firehouse can't say enough about my muffins."

Drew's expression relaxed at that. His mouth twisted into a wry grin. "And who can blame the poor fellows?" he rasped, flashing her a flirty look.

"Drew!" she scolded. "I'm being serious." At least she was trying to be, though she couldn't help flushing, grinning, and feeling altogether good about his coy comment.

"I am too!" His eyes were wide with mock innocence. "I'm sure your muffins are positively exquisite. And I can vouch for your pie firsthand."

"Unless everyone was just making that up at dinner, about how much they liked it."

"I assure you, Molly, they weren't. No one gorges themselves on peach pie just to be polite."

"So featuring baked goods . . . I really think that will

bring the business around." She stopped talking and looked up at him. For some reason she couldn't quite read the expression on his face. "But you're thinking something else." She paused. "Are you thinking that maybe the things I bake aren't good enough to make a difference?"

"No, no." He shook his head. "They're . . . um . . . great. I think—I think it's a good step in the right direction. But, well, I'm just wondering . . . do you think there's a simpler way? Won't all that baking be a lot more work for you? And more costly too?"

"Probably." She sat up, crossing her arms over her chest once more, steeling herself for the task at hand. "But, if it saves the café . . . well, then, it'll be worth it."

"Quite true," he murmured. "Quite true."

"You know, that's one of the things I like about you."

"About me?"

"Yeah." Now that she'd blurted that out, she suddenly felt slightly shy. She wasn't totally comfortable sharing her feelings, especially since she didn't know exactly how the Englishman felt about her. But then, trying to keep her feelings to herself? That was even harder still. "You're such a good listener," she continued. "And that's what I need most. Not judgment, or someone giving their opinion all the time. You're so great that way. You listen and you focus on the positive."

"I do?" He blinked.

"Yes, you do. So many times guys bulldoze their way into your life and tell you everything that's wrong and how to change it and that they're always right and know everything about everything and—"

She could feel herself getting carried away and was almost glad when Drew put his hand on her knee and stopped her mild ranting.

"Maybe they're just trying to help, Molly."

She could feel herself soften at his touch, her hands sliding to her lap. "I don't know. Maybe. But it doesn't often feel that way."

"It doesn't?"

"Not really."

"Hmm." He shifted in the seat, sliding closer toward her. "And would there be any of those sorts of guys in your life presently? What I mean to say is . . . is there, uh, anyone I should consider as competition? Bulldozers or otherwise?"

"No." She laughed out loud. "There's no one."

"Good," he said quietly.

Reaching out, he took both of her hands into his. The incredible feel of him made her wonder . . . how could she already feel so attached to him? So intoxicated by his mere hands holding hers?

She smiled at him curiously. "May I ask you a question?"

"Are you going to hold me down and kiss me till I tell you everything?"

"We *are* in a rowboat."

"I'm happy to paddle like a madman over to that grassy bank." He inclined his head to the side of the lake.

"Please? I've answered two of your questions. Can you at least answer a little one of mine?"

Intentionally, she gazed at him with wistful, pleading eyes that she hoped he'd find irresistible. Evidently it

worked; she saw a flicker of helpless surrender mir-
rored in his.

"Of course," he said softly, amiably. "Of course, I
can." Then he sucked in his breath like a man preparing
for a blow to the stomach. "What is it you'd like to
know?"

"Well, don't get me wrong. I mean, I know it's none
of my business . . ."

"But . . ." He chuckled.

"But . . ." She gave him a crimped smile. "Sam said
something the other day. I wasn't quite sure how to
take it."

His arched brows urged her to go on.

"She said something about not knowing how long
you'd be here. And I thought it was strange because you
and Blake are just starting a business, aren't you? Did
she mean you might have business clients to take care
of out of town?"

"Business out of town?" He sat back, his hands drifting from hers. "Yes, yes, that is a distinct possibility.
There, uh, there may be *some* business out of town."

"Oh, well. I was just wondering. Because to be quite
honest with you, I'm just getting to know you, but if
you're not planning to stay, I wouldn't want to, you
know . . ." Her voice trailed off.

Suddenly she felt self-conscious. Maybe he'd think
she was being too serious or direct, blurting that out.
But she couldn't help it. Something had stirred inside
her the day she met Drew Dawson, and she knew she
wanted to keep getting to know him better. But if he
wasn't staying long-term in Somersby, putting herself

out there just wasn't smart. In fact, coupled with her business problems at the moment, it was downright senseless.

But he sounded like he'd be sticking around Somersby. And the thought of it made her smile. "Of course if you're not leaving, that's good."

"Good?" He wagged his head, a glint of playfulness sparking in his eyes. "Just good? That's all my being here in Somersby rates?"

"Oh . . . uh . . ." There was that devilish look of his, making her feel weak and off balance. "Make that . . . very good."

Her words seemed to dash his spirit a bit. He looked a little less than thrilled.

"Okay, okay," she said, already missing the pleased look in his eyes, the taunting of his smile. "I rate it as 'superior.' Superior and excellent," she answered resolutely, like a queen dubbing a knight—a knight she was falling crowned head over jeweled heels for.

"Much better," he said.

He got up from his seat and her breath caught in sweet anticipation as he made his way closer to her. But his shifting weight threw the small boat off kilter. Tipping right and then left, Drew swayed, attempting to get his bearings. Finally the rowboat tipped completely over, throwing them both into the lake's sun-warmed water.

The surprise plunge had them both laughing when they came up for air. Squealing and yelping, they splashed one another giddily as they stood in the four-foot-deep water. It wasn't long before their ruckus had stirred up a chorus of dogs. Barks and yips began echoing through the neighborhood. Porch lights from several nearby houses flicked on.

Drew's voice lowered to a stage whisper. "Shame on you, Molly Katz, for causing such a row at this late hour. And in such a quiet, lovely suburban neighborhood too."

"Me?" she hissed quietly. "You're the one who started it." She whipped another armful of water at him.

He stepped forward and she attempted to move away, thinking he might try to dunk her. But he caught up with her, and before she knew it, he swooped her up in his powerful arms. He carried her out of the lake, dripping wet, but happy and snug against his chest, thrilled and breathless by his caress.

Chapter Seven

Sam and Blake were already sitting at the kitchen table the next morning when Drew made his way downstairs. From the looks of them, he couldn't tell which of the pair had had the rougher night. Sam had a cotton robe knotted around her waist, half of her blond hair in a floppy ponytail, the other part drooping listlessly around her shoulders. Blake was in a worn T-shirt and cargo shorts, dark gray circles under his eyes. Both held steaming mugs in their hands. Both seemed to be staring into space. His entrance into the kitchen barely registered on them.

"Wow! You two look—" He didn't want to say what he was thinking. Blake ended up saying it for him.

"Bloody terrible?"

"Well, let's just say you've both looked better." He glanced at Sam. "I mean, you *always* look better. Incredibly wonderful. All the time. Truly you do."

His bumbling made her smile. "Believe me, I've felt better too. Amazing what one night without sleep can do."

"I suspect this wasn't a pleasurable night without sleep?" he asked the dazed-looking couple.

Blake shook his sleepy, shaggy head. "Little Em is sick. Been up with a fever all night. And a sick tummy."

"She's finally asleep," Sam explained. "Hopefully for a little while. Poor thing was so miserable." She got up from her chair, and checked the simmering teapot on the stove. "Would you like some more tea, honey?" She glanced at Blake. "The water's still hot."

"No thanks, love. I'm fine." Blake raked his fingers through his unkempt hair. "But I'd be glad to make an omelet for you. What do you think? Would you like one?"

She bent over his chair, kissing the top of his head. "I think you should save your energy, Chef Dawson. But thank you anyway."

It was amazing for Drew to see the two of them, tired as they were, so thoughtful of one another. But then why would it be a surprise? They'd been acting that way ever since he'd arrived in Somersby. Always so conscious of each other's needs, always there for one another. And still so loving and affectionate. At first, he had to admit it had seemed a bit much. Sometimes even slightly nauseating. But now, after the time he'd spent with the two of them, it seemed the norm. In fact, he realized as he watched them that if they behaved in any other way, it'd be completely disturbing.

"Drew?" Sam's voice brought him out of his thoughts. She stood facing him with a coffeepot in her hand.

"Yes?"

"Would you like some coffee?"

"Thank you, yes. But I can get it."

"Nonsense. I'm already up." She turned, retrieved an oversized navy mug out of the cupboard and filled it. He thanked her as she placed the cup before him.

"Speaking of coffee, did you say anything to Molly last night, bro?" Blake leaned forward, looking anxious to know.

Drew sat back in his chair and sighed, rubbing his hand over his forehead. "I just couldn't."

"I know it's dicey, man," his brother said to him. "But you've got to tell her."

"I was. I mean, I want to. But then she started talking last night. She's got this thing—this notion—a very strong notion, mind you, about men. Or boyfriends. Or, I don't know, any male I suppose. She has a problem with them telling her what to do . . . giving her their opinion on things."

Sam's face brightened. She looked amused and chuckled. "And you're finding that difficult? A woman who knows her own mind?"

"Definitely!" he blurted out, and then backpedaled, not wanting to sound chauvinistic or insensitive. "Granted, it's quite an admirable trait indeed. The woman is all about character. And quality. And forthrightness, if that's a word. And quite beautiful on top of it all . . ." He shook his head, barely able to believe it. "But in this situation it is absolutely, undeniably, irrevocably difficult."

"Well, Drewster," Blake said, rubbing his stubbled

chin thoughtfully. "I think you have to make a decision about what's more important."

Drew almost had the brimming mug to his mouth. He stopped in midsip, placing the cup back on the table. "How's that?"

"Is it about her? Her business—her future—is that what's more important?" his brother asked. "Or is it about you? As in you making yet another conquest?"

"Well, I—"

The questions stopped him cold. Is that how his brother viewed his relationship with Molly? Is that how he viewed it himself? As another conquest?

He'd whisked her out of the water last night, his heart pounding and feeling so full, the same way it felt sometimes when he stood on top of a snowy mountain before flying down it. Excited. Nervous. Awed. He'd felt it all with her. And sitting there with her, wrapped in a blanket left behind by some picnickers . . . had he ever quite felt that way before?

"Oh, man, don't put it that way. Do I have to make a choice?" He grimaced. "I'm just thinking there must be a way around this. You won't believe what she's thinking now."

"What?" Sam and Blake asked simultaneously, sitting up in their chairs, looking suddenly more perky and awake.

"Obviously, she still has no clue about the coffee. She thinks her baked goods are the problem."

"Problem?" Blake blinked.

"But they're delicious!" Sam exclaimed.

"Exactly." Drew flung out his arms in despair. "So,

she's thinking the problem is that she hasn't featured them enough. Now she wants to bake like crazy, like some kind of zealous, overachieving Keebler elf, which will mean more work and additional expense."

Sam and Blake both sank back in their chairs, looking just as fatigued as before.

"Oh, gosh." Sam sighed.

"Hmmph." Blake shook his head.

"I know exactly what you mean." Drew nodded.

They all sat in slumped silence for a while till Sam snapped her fingers. "I know!" She sat up in her chair. Her outburst brought Drew and Blake to attention. "*You* need to help her!" she told Drew.

"I beg your pardon?" Drew knew he was looking at her as if she'd lost half her mind, though he was trying hard not to. "Help her bake? Me?"

"Not bake exactly. But just be there, at the café. Tell her you popped in because you knew she'd need extra help once in a while since she'll be busy baking. Then when she's in the kitchen area, investigate the coffee urns. Make new pots of coffee. That way if and when customers do come in, they'll get a taste of some good stuff." She sat back, pleased with herself. But while Drew was still trying to digest her suggestion, she sat up abruptly, biting her lower lip. "You do know how to make decent coffee, don't you?"

"Honestly, it's about the only thing I do know how to make."

"Great." She beamed.

"Ah." Blake gazed at his wife proudly. "It takes the devious mind of a beautiful woman to solve great matters such as these, doesn't it?" He gave an exaggerated quirk of his eyebrows, looking mysterious himself.

"I'm not devious." Sam nudged his shoulder with a soft fist.

Blake chuckled. "Love, don't get me wrong. I adore that dark, unknown side of you."

"My what?" She wagged her head at him, her eyes twinkling.

Drew pretended not to hear their banter or see them kiss as he picked up the morning paper from the table and sorted through it for the sports section.

Yes, he could possibly stop by the café tomorrow after his and Blake's appointment. At least Sam's idea was worth a try, wasn't it? He'd be as charming with Molly as he possibly could, and try to work his way behind the counter to help her. Of course, he didn't know how one pot of coffee would manage to solve the café's overall coffee problem, but maybe it would lead to something. Maybe Molly would see him making it and notice something he does differently from her. That was a possibility. Heaven only knew how she went about concocting the horrible stuff!

Okay, okay. He would definitely pay her a visit tomorrow, he decided. Glancing up, he started to make the announcement to Sam and Blake, but they were still flirting with each other like lovesick teenagers. He had to smile in spite of himself. They were so good with one another. Great role models, those two.

And tomorrow I'll be helping Molly the same way they help each other.

The thought went right to his stomach, making it feel

funny and quivery. Not a totally negative feeling. But not a completely positive one either. Rather a strange, indescribable one.

What's wrong with me anyway? he wondered, staring at the National League baseball stats, but not really seeing them. For being such a noncommittal guy, he sure had been stacking up commitments lately.

For years, he'd never really planned his days—or his nights—or the people he spent them with. He simply took the hours of the day as they came and whoever drifted in and out of his life was quite fine with him.

But now . . .

He told Blake he'd stay longer in Somersby to meet with more prospective clients. He'd committed to rock-climbing with Ryan a full week in advance, something quite foreign from his previous lifestyle where he'd done everything spontaneously. And though he'd been keeping it a secret from her, he was also totally committed to helping Molly make her business a success.

Molly . . . who was on his mind day and night and every second in between.

In truth, she was the real reason he'd told Blake he'd stay longer though he'd never told his brother exactly how long "longer" was. And she was the reason he was dreading the commitment he'd made to his father even more than before.

And then I went and acted totally foolishly, lying to her.

Well, he hadn't totally lied to her. He just hadn't exactly been forthcoming, had he? But then, what was he supposed to say? When she'd asked him about whether he was leaving Somersby or not, it'd taken him totally

by surprise. What should he have done—blurted out
the entire retirement-shoe boutique scenario whereby
she'd say she didn't want to spend as much time with
him then?

She made it clear that's what her answer would be.
And he couldn't exactly blame her. Why keep investing
time and feelings if there wasn't a future in it?

*Wait a minute. Future? Feelings? Did I really just
think that? I truly am in a quandary here, aren't I?*

He slumped down in the chair, totally vexed, the
newspaper caving in on itself in his hands. It was true.
He cared for Molly in a way that he'd never experienced before. For some inexplicable reason, she wasn't
just another conquest to him. And when she questioned
him, well, he didn't even want to think about the possibility of not seeing her again. The evening had gone so
well, he didn't want to face any other reality except for
the one of being with her in that time and place.

So he'd glossed over her inquiry last night, leading
her to believe that there was no other option he was
considering. He'd skirted the entire issue, letting her
think that he hadn't left things open-ended with Blake
and Sam at all, and that Sam could have only been re-
ferring to out-of-town clients that he and Blake might
develop in the future.

There was no way he could face telling her that "out
of town" really meant out of state, as in nine hundred
miles away in Boston. He didn't want to say it because
even he didn't want to hear it.

It's not that he wanted to lead her on or hurt her. The
bloody truth of the matter was, he didn't want to hurt

himself. Who knew he'd meet someone like her at a time like this? The only time in his life when he—Mr. Footloose and Fancy Free—had already made a prior commitment to his parents?

But didn't it just figure? It was all rotten timing, the lot of it.

So he'd just kept quiet with Molly, hoping in the days and weeks to come that something would give way. Telling her last night would've risked too much, would've meant taking a chance that he'd never get to know her better. Never get to hold her close again . . .

Of course . . . once she found out he'd withheld information, she probably wouldn't want to have much to do with him anyway.

How abominably insane! Here I've found the one person I want to be completely honest with—and I feel I have to be totally deceptive to keep her!

The quivery feeling he'd been experiencing in the pit of his stomach tightened into a knot. Ach! This commitment business was much more complicated than he'd ever imagined. No wonder he'd never been up for it before. No wonder he found himself questioning how long he could keep at it.

Opening the café's door, Drew's senses immediately went into overload. First there was the mouthwatering aroma of baked apples and cinnamon, and then the pleasure of seeing Molly, sitting at one of the high oak tables. In her lacy cream shell, pink bibbed apron, and denim skirt, she was a super sweet treat all by herself.

He loosened his tie—actually Blake's tie, lent to him

so he'd look more professional for their appointments that morning—as he strode in the door.

"Hey!" he greeted her, something inside making him wonder how it would feel to do this every day.

"Hey, yourself," she said in that purring way of hers, her smile warming him. "This is a nice surprise."

"For me too," he told her. "Blake and I finished earlier than we expected."

"So . . ." She cocked her head and gazed at him. "I'll bet you think you have the answer, don't you?"

Her question stopped him short. The hardwood floor went silent, no more squeaking beneath his step. Gulping, he stared back at her.

Had she been waiting for him to come in and tell her what he really thought about her business? She did have that uncanny knack for reading his mind. Maybe she knew he'd been thinking something but had refrained from saying it.

"Well, yes, I guess," he stammered. "I mean, I have been thinking about it, and—"

He wanted to tell her the truth. He needed to tell her, and get this thing taken care of between them. If he could just be honest, and not lose her in the process, they could work together to get her business back on track. Then their relationship would be stronger. And then he could move on to tackling the other information he was withholding from her—the "out of town" issue.

But . . .

What if it was a trick? Maybe she was testing him to make sure he wasn't one of those bulldozer chumps she'd dated before. Those know-it-alls she detested and sent out of her life. He didn't want to be shooed away. He wanted to be here with her . . . with Molly, the lady with the strawberry-blond hair, framing a face that a guy could never tire looking at. Molly. With her sensational, glossy lips, huge emerald eyes, and a dab of flour right on the tip of her sweet nose.

"Been thinking about what?" She chuckled. "I haven't even given you the clue yet."

"Oh, right." He swallowed hard, pushing back words he was about to say, words that needed to be said, attempting to key in on her train of thought. "Right. The clue."

What clue?

"I'm waiting for some apple crisps to come out of the oven, and thought I'd rest for a second." She picked up a pencil and a folded sheet of newspaper from the table. "So you're just in time. I'm stuck on twenty-five across. The clue is two words to describe coffee."

She was talking about the answer to a crossword puzzle? Whew, that was close! He wiped the beads of sweat that had formed on his brow since walking into the place.

"In fact, I can get you a cup of coffee, if you'd like. Kind of help you think a little?" She offered with a smile.

"No!" he half-shouted. "I mean, no, thank you." He waved a hand at her. "Had way too much today."

"Okay, then, Mr. Java, you'll have to work from memory. Thinking about coffee, let's say, my coffee . . ." She grinned. "In two words, eleven letters, how would you describe it?"

Bloody awful! The thought came to him in a millisecond.

He looked over at her, his face instantly heated again. Thank goodness, she couldn't *really* read his mind. *Or could she?*

"I, uh, I have to think. Two words, you say?"

"Eleven letters." She nodded, glancing back to the puzzle. "Oh!" She put pencil to paper. "I just got twenty-one down. That helps. Okay, the first word begins with the letter *M*."

"How about—"

Muddy waters. The words came to mind in a flash while she sat staring at him, waiting for a brilliant answer, he was sure. But his brain wasn't exactly cooperating. Though it was running rampant. *Muddy waters. Mucky lattes. Murderous. No, too short. Ghastly grounds. No, too long. Starts with M, eleven letters.*

"How about what?" she asked perkily when he hadn't said anything for a while.

"I'm thinking. I'm thinking." And he was. He just wasn't thinking anything he could say out loud.

"Oh, wait. I think I have the last word." She scribbled on the paper. "Yes. The last word is 'brew.' "

Brew? As in deathly brew?

He couldn't stand it any longer. "Molly. Can we talk?"

"Oh, got something on your mind?" She giggled at him. "And let's see . . ." She tapped the pencil's eraser on her creamy cheek, as if trying to remember something. "Does that mean I have to hold you down and kiss you so you'll tell me every little thing?"

Kiss me? Oh, why did she have to go and say that?

Suddenly he remembered the feel of having her next to him as they cuddled last night, the blanket wrapped around them, the flower-fresh scent of her close and mesmerizing. And, the sound of her voice . . . the most pleasant thing he'd ever heard. He recalled their giggling together, and their whispers floating into a night that seemed to be theirs alone. And the stars . . . he even still had a vision of exactly what the stars looked like as they gazed at them together.

And all the while the life he'd known seemed to fade farther and farther away. Dimmer and dimmer, like a faraway star that was beginning to lose its glow.

No, he couldn't tell her about the coffee right this minute. He couldn't stand the thought of losing what they had just started to share. He didn't want her to think he was another pompous, know-it-all guy. That's not what he wanted her to think of him at all.

But think of her, man, his conscience scolded. *Do you want her to have to work harder? All the while thinking she's on the right track, when you have an easy answer all along?*

But she'll hate me for it, he answered back. *I'll just take it slower. Do it Sam's way. Get in the café and help, till the time is right.*

Time? She's running out of time. Be a mench and tell her!

"Molly, I just think—"

The timer buzzed in the kitchen before he finished his sentence. Molly hopped up from the chair. "Hold that thought, would you?" She darted for the oven in the back room, while he stood frozen waiting for her. She returned in a matter of minutes.

"Gosh, Drew, I can't tell you how glad I am you stopped in." She rolled her eyes. "Really I am. Mr. Mulligan usually makes his round in the mornings," she explained. "Sometimes the afternoons get really long around here even though I have been busy baking a lot today."

"The pleasure is all mine. Totally." He gave her a slight bow which brought a smile to her lips, a smile that encouraged him to go on. This was his window of opportunity to make Sam's suggestion good. "And I thought perhaps with all that baking, you could use some help."

With a delicate touch, he ran his finger over the tip of her nose. He couldn't help it. "A smudge of flour," he told her.

"Oh, I probably look like a mess." She tugged at her braid.

"Yes, you do look like a mess," he said, and waited till a startled look crossed her face before adding, "A very lovely one."

She laughed just as he'd hoped. "Is that supposed to get me back for all the things I've blurted out in the past week?"

"I hadn't thought of it that way. But now that you mention it . . ." He rocked back on his heels. "All right, then." He clasped his hands together. "What can I do to help?"

"Oh, Drew, that's really sweet of you, but as you can

see," she swung out her arms in both directions, "there's not much going on at the moment."

It was true. The cozy café was completely empty. But it didn't matter. He was on a mission. He began rolling up his shirt sleeves.

"How about I wax some furniture? Or, I know," he suggested, feeling a bit underhanded as he did so, "I could make some fresh coffee."

"Hopefully, I'll be able to put your energy and enthusiasm to work soon. But seriously," she said, shrugging her shoulders, "there's nothing you can really do right now. Unless—" She tilted her pretty head, her eyes wide like she wanted to ask something of him. Of course, he was ready to give her anything.

Oh, yeah, anything except for the truth! His conscience nagged at him again.

He immediately tuned out that particular inner voice, and raised his brows. "Unless what?"

"Would you have time to listen to my ideas for the cafe?" She inclined her head toward a quaint table with two chairs.

"Of course I would." Feeling both flattered and apprehensive at the same time, he followed her over to the table.

"Okay. First," she told him excitedly as they sat down, "I've decided to put an ad in the community paper. At first, I thought about advertising in the *Post*, but it's too expensive. And besides, I really just need to target the people in this general area."

"Makes good sense," he agreed, his stomach tightening as it had been this morning. She looked so eager and hopeful . . . and altogether beautiful.

"And did you see the sign in the window when you came in?" she asked him, her eyes bright.

"Actually, yes. Yes, I did."

"Oh, good. I was hoping it was the right size and visible."

"It said something about—" Oh, bloody heck. What had the sign said? He wanted to remember to make her feel good. He'd only glanced at it. It said—ah, yes! "your wonderful muffins. 'Buy one, get one free.' Am I right?"

How he wanted to be right for her, for her sake.

"Exactly." She smiled, and he felt relieved and pleased, and like he could breathe again.

"I'm also going to take some of my baked goods to church so people can sample them. You know how they have coffee and sweets sometimes after service?"

"That's great! Excellent idea!" he commended her and was rewarded with a warm look of gratitude from her lovely eyes.

"And then my *big* idea—" Her grin was so uncontained and wide, he found himself smiling.

"I'm listening." He nodded eagerly.

"I know, and it's so sweet of you."

"I want to, Molly. Truly. What's your big idea?"

"I'm going to approach one of the town's food critics."

He felt his smile retreat, his lips tighten. "Excuse me. Could you, uh, repeat that?"

"Sure. I'm thinking it would be good. Well, at least I hope I'd get a positive review. But, well, maybe if I have one of the local food critics come and sample my baked goods, I'd get a great write-up and the café would get plenty of traffic from it. The thought came to me when I was brushing my teeth this morning, and—" she paused long enough to take a breath, "—at this point it can only help things, right? I mean, what can it hurt?"

Food critic samples baked goods, loves them. That's a good thing. Food critic samples baked goods, loves them, and chases them down with horrific, incredibly evil-tasting coffee. Bad thing. There goes the good write-up, on comes the humiliation.

How awful and embarrassing would it be for Molly to see the truth in print, having it written up in black and white for the entire Somersby County population to see. She might prefer a listener and not a teller, but she had to know, and *he* had to tell her.

"Molly—"

"Yes?"

"Before you go on, there's something I need to say." He knew he sounded serious and he hated to. Especially when her face was all lit up, glowing with hope eternal.

"What is it?"

You're doing good, man, his conscience encouraged. *Now tell her!*

"I, uh, you see—there's—" he sputtered.

Be a man. Be a man. You can do this.

"Yes?"

Tell her now, you yellow-bellied. . . .

"There's a problem . . ."

The glimmering shine began to dim in her great big beautiful green eyes.

"What problem?"

Just tell her and get it over with, will you?

I can't! Those green eyes of hers are starting to look sad. I can't stand it when she looks that way.

So tell her and then tell her how to fix the problem.

She doesn't like guys butting in, remember? She likes listeners.

You're such a coward. So hopeless.

I need more time.

And I told you before, she's running out of it.

I know, I know. You don't have to say it again.

"There's a problem with making the 6:50 showing of the movie you wanted to see tonight. Would you like to go to the 8:10 instead?"

She laughed. "*That* is not a problem, Drew. That's fine."

Chicken! Bwock, bwock, bwock.

I'll tell her later. Soon, I swear.

Sure you will, man. Sure you will.

He really did need a little more time. Time to figure out his feelings for her . . . and time to feel more secure about her feelings for him. It would all be okay—when the time was right.

Right?

Chapter Eight

"And here I thought I was the only man in your life." Mr. Mulligan winked at her from where he sat on the café's cushioned stool. Dressed in his customary short-sleeved shirt and khaki pants, his lined eyes twinkled briefly with a youthful vitality. But his cane lying over the stool next to him told another tale.

"Have you been feeling okay, Mr. Mulligan?" Molly asked, studying him. It seemed to her he'd been looking a little pale lately.

"There you go trying to change the subject." He rolled his eyes.

"No, honestly, I'm not trying to change the subject." She chuckled. "I'm just asking. You look sort of peaked, and you barely touched your coffee and orange juice."

"Nothing to worry about." He waved a wrinkled hand at her. "My stomach has just been acting up. But growing old ain't for sissies. I can handle it," he assured

103

her. "Besides, think I'd quit now and leave you all to him? To an Englishman?"

She laughed, wagging a finger at him. "Actually you'd better stick around for a good long time. I don't know what I'd do if I didn't see you everyday. You're very special to me," she told him candidly. "You know that, don't you?"

"Music to my ears, dear girl." His thin lips crinkled into a smile. "Music to my ears." He paused and let out an exaggerated sigh. "Well, go ahead. You might as well tell me all about him. You're dying to, aren't you?"

All smiles, Molly nodded eagerly, feeling so glad to tell him—someone, anyone—about Drew. Flinging her arms in the air, feeling slightly out of control, she felt giddy just talking about him. "Well, I don't know. He's just so . . . and he makes me feel so . . . and, well, everything between us is so—"

The older man burst out laughing about that. "You've got a bad case of it, don't you?"

"Yes!" she proclaimed. "Yes, I do. Oh, and it's so nice because his brother Blake and sister-in-law Sam are so, so awesome," she told him. "We have such a good time with them. And my friend April—you've met her before—"

"Long dark hair? Big, big brown eyes?"

Her eyes narrowed at his selective memory. "You don't miss a thing, do you?"

"Molly girl, I'm old and ancient, not blind or dead."

"Well, April and her husband are good friends with Blake and Sam too. It's great. We all get together and have dinner as couples. Like tonight, we're all meeting at Blake and Sam's for dinner. It's easier that way with their daughter Emma and all."

"I remember those days," Mr. Mulligan replied wistfully. Turning his head away from her for a moment, he seemed to be looking back at years gone by. "Oh, to be young and in love!" he sighed.

Love?

The word brought her to attention. Her back straightened. Her eyes blinked double-time. The hairs on the back of her neck bristled.

"Oh, well, Mr. Mulligan," she sputtered, "I never said . . . I mean, I didn't say I was in *love*," she stressed the word.

He cackled at that. "Believe me, Molly girl, from the look in your Eire green eyes, you didn't have to."

"Yes, but . . ."

Love? Just because she wanted to talk about the new British guy in town? About how wonderfully incredible he was? And how he made her feel this funny, crazy way inside?

Just because thoughts of the Englishman seemed to rise in her heart with the sun. And make her feel content and dreamy as she settled down to sleep?

And because the sight of him could make her shiver and smile even though her business was doing horribly, and she was truly exhausted from trying so hard to save it?

Did all those things add up to *love?*

"Do you have my muffins ready for the boys at the station?" Her older friend interrupted her thoughts.

"Huh?"

"My bag of muffins? For the guys at the station?"

"Oh . . ." She came to attention, her voice turning instantly stern. "Yes, I do, as a matter of fact. But I'm not going to keep giving them to you if you're going to keep paying for them."

Fiddling with his watch, holding it up to his ear, checking to make sure it was still ticking, her elderly friend pretended not to hear her correctly. "What's that? Don't know what you're talking about."

"Mr. Mulligan . . ." Crossing her arms, she tapped her foot, waiting for the truth.

"Mr. Mulligan what?"

"Don't act so innocent. You know exactly what I mean. Somehow I always find money wherever you've been sitting." She arched her brows, daring him to deny it. "And you know what our deal is, sir. You help me out behind the counter when I need it. I give you muffins when you're paying a visit to your buddies."

"Oh, well, that. You're getting all excited over nothing," he told her as he took his time getting down from the wooden stool. "It's not a payment. It's a tip." He picked up his cane from the nearby stool and waved it. "And I'm allowed to leave you a tip, aren't I?" He appeared totally offended. "What? Do you think I'm a poor man or something? Is that it? You feel sorry for me?"

Molly shook her head, smiling at his theatrics. "You are so stubborn. Stubborn and willful, you know that?"

She started packing up his muffins, while he grinned proudly and cackled all over again. "Pretty much!" he admitted. "But," he said as she handed him the bag of goodies and he ambled toward the door, "it takes one to know one, dear heart. Takes one to know one."

And with that, Mr. Mulligan made his way out the door. But his words taunted her for a while longer, even while she was cleaning up after him and found a five-dollar tip underneath his muffin plate.

"Sam, can I help you with anything?"

Molly peeked her head into the kitchen where Sam was scurrying back and forth making the last of the dinner preparations. Blake was in there, too, wearing a bibbed apron decorated with Emma's handprints in primary colors. Holding Emma in his arms, he looked like Molly felt—willing to do something, but not sure what.

"Are you kidding?" Sam answered her, tucking her blond hair behind her ears. "You made the pasta salad and the dessert. More than your fair share. And," she said, surveying the kitchen, "I think we're in pretty good shape. The beans are in the oven. The salad is ready." She pointed at the stove and refrigerator respectively.

"I just checked the ribs and chicken," Blake added. "As soon as they're done grilling, we'll be ready to eat."

"Thank goodness. I'm starving," Drew piped up, suddenly standing right behind Molly in the threshold. "I thought this was some new kind of torture you'd cooked up for me, big brother. No pun intended of course," he added, laying his arm around her shoulder casually, easily, in a way that made her feel close to him. It amazed her that his simplest touch could bring her so much pleasure.

"So you admit the rock climbing took it out of you today, huh?" Blake smirked at Drew.

"Not at all. I'm in completely fine shape," he replied, drawing Molly closer against his fit form till she almost seconded the statement.

"I suppose our friend Ryan didn't fare as well." Blake's eyes gleamed with amusement.

Sam looked up from counting out forks and knives. "April said he only made it as far as the couch. Passed out from fatigue and she couldn't wake him. Even clanged pots and pans in his ears. But he's down for the count for the evening."

They all laughed at the image, and Molly was sure they were all remembering the previous weekend when Ryan had been downing two generous slices of pie while declaring that rock climbing would be a piece of cake.

"Not like our Drew here, right, Princess?" Blake said to his daughter resting in his arms.

"Dew?" she answered in her sweet voice, reaching out for her uncle to take her.

Molly looked back at Drew and saw his eyebrows arch in surprise—surprise and the slightest bit of apprehension.

"Dew?" Emma repeated.

Watching his handsome face, Molly saw Drew's features go instantly soft at the sound of Emma's voice. "Ah, you little heart melter, you," he said, clearly affected, moving away from Molly for the moment and holding out his hands to his niece. "Come to your Uncle Drew."

Blake turned over Emma Corinne to his brother

while explaining to Molly, "She just started walking a little while ago. But by this time of day, she tires herself out and wants to be held."

Looking at Emma, nestled against Drew's chest, being hugged in his muscular arms, Molly thought wistfully how she wished she could trade places with the little one. In the midst of all that gentleness, Drew Dawson had never looked more masculine to her.

"I also think she's still getting over that flu virus too," Sam chimed in, while grabbing salad dressing from the refrigerator. "For a summer virus, it's been really quite rough. I've heard many people, young and old, have had a tough time shaking it completely. A few people at the agency were out with it for days. Thank goodness Blake and I didn't get it." Her eyes glanced heavenward.

"Whatever the reason Emma wants to be held, I don't mind a bit," Drew spoke up. "I'm happy to hold her," he said, pulling his head back so Emma's was looking up at him. "Little girl, what say we go outside where we have room to play. Okay?" He rubbed noses with his niece. Then looking at Molly, he added, "Want to play too?"

As he said the words, his boyish smile was so inviting and adorable, and totally mischievous, she couldn't have resisted if she'd wanted to. "Sam, I can take these plates outside and set the table," she offered.

"Oh, thanks, Moll, that'd be great."

After Sam loaded her up with dinnerware, Molly followed Drew and Emma out the door leading to the patio and backyard. Since it was still early evening, the patio had a different look to it than she remembered from the last weekend. Last Saturday, she'd arrived later and by then dusk had settled in. Torches had already been lit, and stars were starting to dot the skies overhead.

But this evening, with plenty of daylight left, she could appreciate the patio's inviting look and the brightly colored flowers that greeted her, mostly over-sized pots and baskets of impatience and petunias. A handful of birds scattered from the copper-topped bird-house when the three of them walked out the back door.

Drew carried Emma over to the grass, making a lap for her with his outstretched legs. His legs looked tan and muscular, at least the part Molly could see sticking out from under his shorts. She tried not to be too dis-tracted by them as she went to work setting the table, looking up every now and then to see Drew entertain-ing his darling niece. With one arm around Emma, he used his free hand to pluck a dandelion stem from the ground. Emma giggled as he blew at the wispy clump of dandelion seeds, and the light-as-a-feather pieces went floating off in the air.

It was all Molly could do to make small-talk, espe-cially when her mind was racing, involuntarily conjur-ing up all sorts of images in her head: domestic images of her and Drew, and maybe even a child or two of their own. She couldn't help trying different scenarios on for size, seeing how they fit.

And that's when it hit her. Struck her with such a force, her hands stopped folding the yellow paper nap-kins, and her entire body surged with a flash of heat.

Her mouth fell open, and her eyes went wide, locking on Drew's face.

I've got to be careful. I'm really falling for this guy. Maybe Mr. Mulligan is right. . . .

Why else would she be thinking of him this way? Why else would she have asked him about staying in Somersby? She wanted more time with him. Lots of it. Time to get to know every last thing about him. If something went wrong now, she'd be devastated. He was so different. Someone who wasn't playing games. Someone who was totally honest and up-front.

Oh, yeah . . . I'm falling for this guy big-time. Her eyes fixed on him.

Drew must've felt her stare. He glanced over, tilting his head. "Are you okay?"

"Me?"

"Yes, you." He laughed. "What are you thinking? You look positively shocked about something."

"Oh, I was just thinking that, um . . ." she stammered. "Thinking how comfortable you seem with Emma," she sputtered, nodding at the two of them.

He chuckled at that. "Trust me, I can see why you'd be surprised. Quite honestly I'm a bit shocked myself." He grinned at Emma who was reaching up with her hand, patting his moving mouth while he talked.

"I've never been around babies or toddlers much. Or any kids at all for that matter. When my older brothers were starting their families," he explained, as he took one of Em's fingers in his and kissed it, "I was off at college or traveling. I admit when I first arrived here, I wasn't all that comfortable about holding a live little body in my arms.

"But now a slightly larger body . . ." he paused, inclining his head at Molly, his glimmering eyes taking her in, "say about a five-foot—how tall are you exactly?" He grinned lasciviously.

"About five-six." She couldn't help but giggle, part of her relishing his flirting. The other part relieved he hadn't known what she'd really been thinking.

"Yes, about five-six is quite a good size. I feel very comfortable with that." He teased, making her cheeks flush. "Although again, not to sound arrogant, but over the course of my stay with Sam and Blake, I've realized I'm not bad with the little ladies either. Am I, Em?"

In fact, he seemed quite at ease, soaring Emma over his head like an airplane while she squealed down at him.

"You might want to watch it," Sam's cheery voice turned their heads as she walked out the patio door, carrying a casserole dish. "She just ate. I'd hate for any of it to come back up on your pullover shirt."

Blake was right behind Sam, his hands also full with the salad bowl. "Drewster, you can put the princess in her walker if you'd like." He nodded to the opposite side of the patio where the walker sat dormant. "She can putter about in that while we're eating."

Drew scooped Emma off the lawn and strapped her into the walker. Meanwhile Blake removed the chicken and ribs from the grill. Sam and Molly made a couple more trips into the kitchen for the rest of the dinner fixings. In a matter of minutes, the four of them were seated at the table, digging into the feast.

"We should try a New England boil sometime, Drew." Blake looked up from his meal to address his brother. "Remember those from the Cape?"

Drew nodded. "Yes. You really should have a go at it, Chef Dawson."

"I can't believe the Labor Day trip to the Cape is coming up so soon," Sam shook her head. "Summer has gone by so quickly." She sighed, before turning to Molly. "But the trip is a good way to end the season. All of Blake's family gets together then. His parents rent out a giant house there."

"Actually you should come too, Molly," Blake invited her. "Really. You'd love it."

She blinked at him, stunned but excited by the invitation. "Me?"

"Yes!" Sam encouraged her. "It would be so much fun for all of us. It'll be my first time too. Oh, and you could be in charge of desserts." Her eyes lit up at the notion.

Molly turned to look at Drew, thinking he'd be prodding her to come along too. But his eyes, she realized, didn't look as bright. "Could you really afford to take time off from the café?" he asked.

Always thinking about her welfare, wasn't he? She sighed at the amazingly sweet man.

Meanwhile on the other side of the table, Blake shrugged. "Other people close their businesses for vacation during the summer. It's not that unusual," he replied.

Molly bit her lip, hating to speak the truth out loud. "Sad to say, I could close for a week and not even lose much money." *Can't lose money you're not making,* she thought to herself.

"Well, think about it," Blake suggested. "The family would love to have you."

She noticed Drew didn't say much. He seemed to be concentrating on his ribs, and leaving the urging to Sam and Blake instead. Maybe he didn't want to be pushy or presumptuous, a quality she really did love about him.

Their dinner conversation was easy and light, and pretty much nonstop until the sound of voices coming from the side yard hit them all at the same time.

"Who could that be?" Blake wondered out loud.

"April and Ryan?" Sam glanced curiously over her shoulder to look.

Blake arched a brow. "Maybe she finally woke him up."

"I'm surprised he didn't skip dinner and wait for dessert," Drew quipped.

As the voices came closer, the two couples waited anxiously. Sam and Blake were both turned around in their chairs, straining to see. Finally, another couple appeared. But it wasn't April and Ryan. It was an older couple, toting suitcases behind them, and they were grinning from ear to ear.

The woman was the first to speak, her voice beyond happy. "Blake!" she exclaimed.

"Mum?" Blake shook his head in disbelief.

"Drew!" the man exclaimed, leaving his suitcase behind and sauntering onto the patio, his hands outstretched.

"Pops?" Drew leaned forward in his chair.

Molly took in the reunion scene, and readily noticed the family resemblance between the brothers and their parents. She also noticed that Blake and Sam appeared totally surprised, but delighted, to see Mr. and Mrs. Dawson. Drew, on the other hand, looked surprised—and uneasy.

After hellos and hugs, and turns holding baby Emma, Molly realized quickly that there was more than a strong family resemblance that the Dawson parents shared with their sons. Right away, she could see where the Dawson brothers had gotten their easygoing dispositions, their sense of humor and ways of making others feel warmed and charmed in their presence. Without a moment's hesitation Edward and Judith Dawson had made her feel that way.

Surveying the food spread on the table, Edward's face lit up. "Ah, barbecued ribs and chicken. Looks like we came on the right night, Judith," he said to his wife as Blake seated them in the patio chairs April and Ryan had occupied the weekend before.

"Trust me, Pops, you would be proud of our Blake," Drew spoke up. "This is not the extent of your son's culinary delights," he nodded to his brother. "Wait until Wednesday."

"Wednesday?" Edward looked blank.

"Blake cooks for us on Wednesdays," Sam explained. "I have a staff meeting that night so he picks up Emma and has dinner ready when I get home."

"Really?" Their mom drawled out the word, her brows arched in an expression closer to shock than surprise. "Blake actually cooks?"

Molly chuckled at that. It seemed they'd finally hit

on a subject that took a moment of Judith's attention off Emma who was settled on her grandmother's lap.

"What kinds of dishes do you prepare, dear?" Judith asked.

Drew looked at Molly, mouthing a "this should be good" at her and grabbed her hand, squeezing it affectionately.

"Well, Mum . . ." Blake took a sip of water. "I make things like, uh, well . . . most recently I made a pot of chili."

Judith's eyes widened. "Chili?" She nodded. "Always a good hearty dinner," she said approvingly. "I'm impressed." She made a funny face at Emma who giggled, before turning back to Blake. "What else?"

"Well, last week I made chili, and then the week before, I made . . . uh . . ." He scratched his scalp as if trying to remember. That's when Sam jumped in.

"You wouldn't believe his chili, Judith. It's the best I've ever tasted. He'll have to make it again this Wednesday so you can taste it."

Judith smiled serenely. "Well, what I've always said it true. Behind every successful man there's a great woman who turns him into the person his mother always knew he could be." Judith winked at Sam, and Molly observed the fond smile Sam gave back to her mother-in-law.

What must it be like? Molly wondered, trying not to feel envious. *To have a husband who looks at you adoringly? And a child that brings so much joy to everyone? Plus a mother-in-law who obviously respects and cherishes you?*

"But unfortunately . . ." Judith started, and all eyes turned to her at the sound of the word, "we won't be here until Wednesday."

"Just here for the weekend, as a matter of fact," Edward said between bites of beans and salad.

"Mum . . . Dad . . ." Blake spoke up, "you know you're welcome to stay longer. For as long as you like."

"Thanks, son." Edward wiped his mouth with a napkin. "But we're simply here for a quick stay. Don't want to impose. But we did want to deliver our important news in person."

No sooner were the words out of his father's mouth than Drew stopped mid-swallow and his glass of water came crashing back down on the table with a noisy thunk. He began coughing so violently that Molly reached out to pat him on the back.

"Are you okay?" she asked.

"Wrong p-pipe," he managed to get out in between gasps, his face reddening.

When Blake realized there was no need to perform the Heimlich on his brother or to call nine-one-one, he turned back to his dad. "What news, Pops?"

"I hate to disappoint everyone," Edward started out, "but we're going to have to cancel the trip to Cape Cod this Labor Day."

"No Cape Cod?" Blake's mouth dropped. "Is something wrong? Are you ill? We always go to the Cape."

Edward shook his head. "I'm fine. But it's apparent that it's not going to work out this year."

"But it's a tradition. It has to work out." Blake looked like a young boy who had just had his dreams crushed.

Molly thought Judith must have thought so too because with a faint smile on her lips, she reached over and patted Blake on the hand. "I'm sorry, dear. But Phillip's firm is sending him to Europe that week, and Cara's doctor said she's too far along in her pregnancy to make the trip."

"What about Colin and Lauren?" Drew asked. Molly looked up at the sound of his voice. Funny, unlike Blake he didn't seem all that upset about the news. *In fact, was that a look of relief on his face?*

"Lauren's grandmother passed," Edward spoke up. "And they went forward with the burial services, but the extended family chose that weekend to meet in Arizona for a service for her."

"What a bloody mess. I suppose it is rather difficult getting us all together, isn't it?" Blake shook his head and sat quietly for a moment, staring at his mother and daughter. "Mum, would you like me take Emma for you? I'm sure you're hungry and would like to eat. I actually can't imagine that she's sitting still in one place so long."

"Yes, Judith. Go ahead and eat," Sam added.

"I'm fine. I can eat anytime. But I can't do this anytime." She snuggled Emma against her, hugging her to her chest. "Of course, maybe I will get to see her again at Christmas. Say in Vail or Tahoe? Your father and I thought perhaps the family could all get together then. We've already started looking for places to accommodate the lot of you." She paused and looked around the table. "That is, if it sounds at all doable."

"We'll meet you wherever and whenever you'd like,

Mum. Whatever works out for the rest of the clan," Blake offered. "I just need to grieve for a moment longer about the Cape." He stuck out his lower lip. "And here, such a shame, we had invited Molly to join us there."

"Oh, Molly, I'm sorry." Judith turned to her, apologizing with a wan smile. "We ruined your plans too?"

Molly shook her head. "No, really, it's fine. It only came up a few minutes ago. It's not as if I'd made any arrangements yet. Honest."

"Yes, Mum. Not to worry," Drew piped up. "Doubtful she was going anyway," he added matter-of-factly, not looking at all disappointed.

As Drew launched into an explanation of Molly's responsibilities at the café with his mother, and while Edward was drawn into a conversation with Sam and Blake, Molly felt like she was staring at a whole new side of Drew. It was as if she didn't know him. But he didn't seem to notice. Because at the moment that's exactly how she felt.

What is it about this trip to Cape Cod? One moment it seemed like he cared about her, was concerned about her and her welfare. And the next moment she'd look at him, and, well, something just didn't strike her right. Was it truly concern he had for her, or had he really not *wanted* her to go to the Cape with them? Did he feel like that made things too serious? Did he have something to hide? Maybe a family secret? Another girlfriend?

She was trying to sort it out in her head, when Drew's mother addressed her. "In any case, I'm glad I had the opportunity to meet you tonight, Molly." Her blue eyes were warm and accepting like she meant it. "How did the two of you meet anyway? Did Blake introduce you?"

"Sort of," Molly replied, looking at Drew.

"And sort of not," he said, smiling at her affectionately in the way she'd grown accustomed to—at least before the subject of the Cape had come up tonight. He put a proprietary arm around her shoulder, making her feel secure and close to him. But at the moment, she felt confused too. "Lucky for me, I bumped into Molly the moment I got off the plane from Boston."

"Oh?" His mom smiled, looking anxious to hear more.

"Pretty much." He nodded.

"What he's not telling you is that I literally knocked into him, spilling hot tea on him before he could even get out of the terminal." Molly winced. "But, Mrs. Dawson—"

"Judith," she interjected.

"But, Judith, you raised him well. He was the perfect gentleman about it."

"A perfect gentleman. Yet she still wouldn't tell me her name." A glint of playfulness shone in Drew's eyes, as his gaze turned from his mother and narrowed in on her.

Molly chuckled. "I didn't know you were interested." She shrugged coquettishly.

"Even though I stood there like a bumbling idiot, staring at the *M* on your purse and guessing what it might stand for?"

"Well, I didn't think we'd actually see each other again."

Judith shifted Emma on her lap, appearing amused and interested in their story. "If you didn't trade names or numbers, how *did* you come to meet again?"

"Actually," Drew tore his eyes away from Molly and turned to his mother, "as fate would have it, the very next morning Blake and I paid a visit to Corner Coffee Café. And there was this green-eyed beauty all over again."

Judith laughed, shaking her head in amazement. "That's a wonderful story," she gushed. "And she finally told you her name?" She winked at Molly.

"Not until approximately our third or fourth date," Drew teased, squeezing Molly's shoulder.

Suddenly their conversation was interrupted by the clinking sound of Edward striking his glass with a fork. All eyes turned to look at him, even little Emma's.

"Does everyone have a glass? I'd like to propose a toast."

"Edward, I don't think—" Judith started, but her husband seemed zeroed in on his own agenda, too oblivious to acknowledge her.

"To our family!" Edward raised his glass, and the others followed suit. "Whether close together or miles apart . . . we are always near, close in heart."

"Here, here!" the Dawson boys sounded off.

"And while we have our glasses raised," Edward continued on, his glass still in the air, "I want to make another toast. A toast of congratulations to a particular member of our family." His eyes landed on Drew.

"Edward, please—" Judith appealed to her husband to stop. But her arms were filled with Emma, and she couldn't move to reach him. Her beseeching eyes pleaded with him, but he didn't seem to notice.

"It's okay, Jude." Edward sloughed off her concern. "I've got it covered. I was going to make the announcement at the Cape anyway."

"An announcement?" Blake looked from his father to his brother. "About Drew?"

"Not now, Edward, please." Judith's voice strained as she tried again.

"Dad, really . . ." Drew's arm dropped from around Molly. He leaned forward trying to stop his father, get his attention. "Mum's right."

"No time like the present, son." Edward nodded sagelike as if he knew what was best. Meanwhile, Molly realized Drew's expression had turned to one of dread. Beads of sweat had formed on his upper lip.

"To Drew." Edward raised his glass, and only Sam, Blake and Molly followed his lead this time. "To my youngest son, who upon my retirement will be taking over the family business next month. I thank you, son, and congratulate you. We'll be glad to have you back home in Boston soon."

Chapter Nine

A dazed silence hovered over the patio table following Edward's toast. But that lasted less than a minute. Then all bedlam broke loose. Blake's tumbler slipped from his hands, glass shattering and flying in all directions, water spilling on him and on the table. Emma burst out wailing, startled by the loud, frightening sound.

Meanwhile, Drew could hear his mom's voice attempting to rise over the clatter, reprimanding her husband, telling him that she'd begged for him to restrain himself, and, as usual, he just couldn't manage to do that, could he? Obviously, his pops wasn't about to keep quiet either. He added to the noise, his tone escalating with his wife's in an effort to defend himself.

But the thing that concerned Drew the most was Molly's response to the whole mess. The look she gave him . . . it was excruciatingly painful; tore his heart out, making him feel sick and hollow inside. How much easier it would've been if she'd been raging mad and started pummeling him. But no, it wasn't anger he saw in her eyes. It was distrust—and hurt. Like she suddenly didn't even know who he was. And then, when it seemed like she couldn't stand to look at him any longer, in the midst of all the chaos, she excused herself. She leaped from her chair and took off running. Where to, who knew?

Probably anywhere that will take her far, far away from me! he imagined.

Her reaction paralyzed him; blinded him to everything around him but the vision of her disappointed face etched in his mind. All he could manage to do was sit stunned and silent in the middle of all the chaos going on around him.

His insides felt raw. His emotions were so jumbled it frustrated him. Without even meaning to, he had betrayed everyone at the table. Everyone. And he'd only meant to help. He certainly hadn't meant to hurt anyone or disappoint them. That hadn't been his intention.

But then, seriously, what did they all expect? Everyone knew what he was like. Was it his fault, really? Was he to blame because he was an amateur at this commitment stuff? An unseasoned participant? He'd been hurled into this mess of people with all their problems and needs. And all of a sudden he was supposed to know how to handle all of it?

His dad wanted a successor. His brother wanted a business partner. Sam longed for more family close by for Emma. Ryan was looking for a friend to hang out with. And then there was Molly. Molly, who wanted someone to be around. Not someone to direct her life, she was strong enough to do that. But someone she could talk to, and more than anything, trust.

That someone could have been him.

Wow! I really botched that up, didn't I? He sank farther back into his chair. *What a bloody mess I've made of everything!* he thought, staring blankly at the people scrambling around him.

. . . And what do you want, Drew?

Huh? Me?

Yes, you. What do you want?

Well, I want . . .

Part of him wanted to run away just like Molly had. But much, much farther away. Like back to California where his buddies and the surf and sun would be there to welcome him . . . or up to Whistler where summer activities were still going on. Anywhere. Just away from all this . . . all of these constraints. All of these people tugging on him.

But then . . .

There was an even greater part of him that could only think about Molly. And couldn't remotely fathom the feeling of being separated from her.

He needed to go after her.

No, that wasn't true.

He *wanted* to go after her.

"We'll talk later," he shouted to his relatives over the uproar.

At the sound of his voice, his mom turned away from the commotion. She seemed to be the only one lucid enough to step outside her feelings and consider anyone else's.

"Drew, go after her," she insisted sternly.

It was a command, but he could tell from her eyes that it came from her heart. It wasn't his mother thinking about good manners and the proper thing to do, it was his mother giving total approval, encouraging him and the inexplicable feelings he had just begun to acknowledge. Deep feelings, taking hold of him, that he couldn't even describe. But ones she seemed to already know existed inside him.

He stood up. "You're right, Mum," he told her. "I have to."

She nodded knowingly, and he knew her well enough to know that it wasn't the moonlight or the candle's glow that was making her look misty-eyed. "Go!" she ordered. "And don't come back till you've found her. Do I make myself clear?"

She certainly did with her commanding voice, her reassuring smile. It was just what he needed. It gave him hope. Hope that things would be all right. He'd search for Molly. And he'd find her. He had to. Because Judith Dawson had always been the only woman he could never say no to. The one female he could never let down.

Till Molly Katz. Till now.

He hadn't meant to knock his chair over as he sprang out of his seat, but he heard it crashing to the ground as he took off and tore to the front of the house. He'd half expected to see Molly pulling out of the driveway, zooming down the street at a hundred and twenty miles per hour away from him. But then he remembered that she hadn't driven over that day. He'd picked her up. And the sheer possibility that she wasn't too far gone yet, possibly still within his reach, filled his chest with hope.

Not that it lasted long. Standing on the sidewalk, looking up and down the street for any sign of her only made his spirit deflate once again. There was no sign of Molly anywhere.

Maybe she's in the house? He turned to look at the two-story home behind him.

But no . . . he knew the look he had seen in her eyes, a look that had made his heart ache. She definitely wanted to distance herself from him. The house was too close, too easy.

That meant there was only one place she could be—the lake. It was easy enough to get there. But, he wondered, as he sprinted through the neighborhood toward the water, how easy would it be to get her to listen to him?

Even the ducks look happy! Molly thought glumly, trying to catch her breath. She'd sprinted block after block through the neighborhood, tears blinding most of her way. Now she stood staring out onto the lake, the tears half-dried on her cheeks, feeling tired, defeated and sad through and through. She shook her head, trying to shake such a ridiculous thought.

Ducks? Looking happy? Had she lost her mind?

But in an odd way, they truly did look happy. Two of the fluffy creatures were swimming side by side in the glow of the moonlight. Another pair looked as if they were doing tricks to entertain one another, bobbing their heads in the water, swishing their tails. They even seemed to be in couples, enjoying their mates. And here she was . . . once again . . . all alone.

Plopping down on the grassy bank, she let out a weary sigh, still not believing what had just happened. How could it be true? How could she have been so foolish? She had really felt like there was something special about Drew Dawson . . . something that seemed so right. Every day growing more and more sure, and then . . . whoa! How could she have been more wrong?

Had she misunderstood their conversation the other night? Why had he lied to her about staying in Somersby? Had she misread the look in his eyes she had thought meant he cared? And the way he touched her and held her in his arms—it had seemed so special. Was he the same way with every other female he met?

The thought crushed her, bringing on tears. She buried her head in her arms, her mind reeling.

Maybe she had been too pushy. Rushing things. Forcing him to say things she wanted to hear. But she'd only asked because she didn't want to get hurt. And here she was . . . feeling hurt.

Or . . . maybe it wasn't her at all. Maybe it was him. Perhaps she didn't *really* know him. Maybe he was the kind of guy who would say anything to any girl at any given time.

"Arrr," she growled out loud, hitting the grassy earth with her hands. The whole thing was so maddening. So frustrating! And not exactly what she needed at the moment when she was already so tired and overwhelmed with her dying business.

Jumping to her feet, she slid cautiously down the bank in her sandals. Spying some smooth stones at the water's edge, she hurled them into the lake with all her might.

"I curse the day I ever met you, Drew Dawson!" she yelled out to the rippling water and to the ducks scurrying to get out of striking distance.

"I hope you hear me!" she yelled, wiping away a stray tear. "I wish—" She heaved a rock into the air, "—I'd—" She slammed another one into the lake. "—never, ever—" She unloaded a few more stones into the pond, "—met you!"

There! Now I feel a little better! she thought to herself, smoothing down her silky turquoise halter top with her rock-free hand. Wiping her tear-stained cheeks dry, she took a deep breath.

Yes, she felt better, but a little silly about her outburst too. And she felt even more ridiculous when a voice startled her from behind. His voice.

"Umm . . . I did hear you. And I was wondering . . . would there be anything I might say to change your thoughts on that particular matter?"

Swinging around to face him, she felt embarrassed beyond words. No doubt he'd seen everything, probably even her tear-rimmed eyes glistening in the moonlight. But then, why should she be embarrassed anyway? He was the one who had lied. He was the one who should be ashamed of himself.

Squeezing the remaining rocks in her hand, her chagrin subsided while her anger began to rise again.

"You're not thinking of throwing those in my general direction, are you?" He smiled weakly.

Honestly, the thought had crossed her mind. "I'll try to restrain myself," she replied curtly. "But as you know, self-control is not my greatest strength."

"We all have our weaknesses."

"And let me guess. One of yours might be the inability to tell the truth?"

He looked totally whipped and frazzled, sweat pouring off of him, his long hair hanging in wet clumps like he'd just run a marathon to get to her. And his eyes were the most heartbreaking thing yet. Dark and downcast, his eyes seemed to show every ounce of worry he was feeling, every apprehensive, unsure thought.

She would've felt sorry for him if she wasn't so darn mad at him.

"Could we, uh, sit down?" he stammered, nodding to a bench up on a grassy area. It seemed his usual self-confidence had eluded him for the moment.

Sit down? Next to him? Admittedly, that didn't make her feel too self-confident either. She wasn't sure she could handle being that close to him, feeling the tension that always existed between them, or knowing there was the possibility that his shoulder or his bare leg might brush up against hers. Or that his pleading eyes might easily knock down the wall she was trying to quickly build around her heart.

"I'd just like to talk to you. Explain everything," he begged. "Please?"

She didn't know what he could possibly say to make things right, but if he was willing to try, maybe he at least deserved the chance to be heard. She dropped the rest of the rocks from her fist, and brushed the dust from her hands.

"Actually, now that you're ready to listen, I'm not sure I know where to begin," he said, once they were seated on opposite ends of the bench.

"Hmmph." She smacked her lips, not wanting to sound so caustic, but not being able to help it either. "How about with the interesting part? You know, the part where you and I were in a rowboat on this very lake, all cozy and sweet, when you lied to me about your business? About staying in Somersby? Of course, I didn't know at the time that you had lied to me," she continued, her words practically tripping over each other, "but now I do. So, you know, if you wouldn't mind starting right there, I wouldn't mind at all. In fact, I'd really appreciate it."

He perched forward on the edge of the bench, his broad back to her. "But it actually goes back further than that." He rubbed his hands together.

A cramping pain flitted across her stomach. "You lied to me before the other night?"

"No, no." He shook his head, turning back to look at her. "And must you use the word *lie*? I didn't exactly lie. It's sounds so ugly and accusatory."

"And accurate?" She arched a brow at him. "I'd say you lied to me and to your brother."

"No, not really," he answered definitively. "Perhaps I didn't reveal the entire truth of the matter, but I am not in the habit of lying. Nor do I intend to start."

"Well, let me just clue you in, Mr. Dawson. In the end, it doesn't really matter what it's called. The outcome feels pretty much the same."

With that, he peered up to the heavens, seemingly searching the stars for answers. Blowing out an exasperated puff of air, he said, "Heaven only knows how I've managed to make such a bloody mess out of everything!"

"Uh . . ." She crossed her arms over her chest. "Heaven knows, and I think you might too, if you thought about it for a minute."

He couldn't help but glare at her. "You really are a tough one, aren't you?"

"I have to be, Drew," she said sternly, but more softly. "My heart's at stake here."

He glared at her like he couldn't believe she'd had the nerve to say such a thing. "And mine isn't?"

The biting tone, the brevity of his words took her aback. Left her breathless and wordless; left her thinking about him for a moment instead of herself. Was he really hurting over this as much as she was? Could he possibly really care as much as she did?

"Look, Molly," he finally said. "Please understand that this thing between Blake and myself, well, he got me to come to Somersby under totally false pretenses to begin with. Never once mentioned this business plan of his till he'd gotten me here. Just the same, I never told him about the situation with our dad because we just hadn't gotten that far." He shrugged as if it all made sense. "And I never assumed it would come up at this point in time. I knew I still had time before we went to the Cape and the big announcement was going to be made. I thought I had plenty of time to address the issue. And furthermore, it has nothing to do with you and me anyway. It's a thing between brothers and something that will work out one way or another."

"Okay." She was trying to understand. "So you thought your brother wouldn't find out about you taking over the family business before the trip to the Cape. But you have to admit, you led him on just like you've been leading me on. Why did you keep going on appointments with Blake?"

"Oh, that's quite easy to explain actually." His hands flung up in the air. "That is entirely your fault."

Her jaw dropped and her eyes narrowed to a squint. *Is he serious? Is he crazy?*

Sitting up poker straight, she leaned into him, shrilling. "All my fault? Drew Dawson, I cannot believe you! You're not straight with your brother. But that's okay, you say, because he wasn't straight with you. But now you're blaming this on me? Do you ever take any of the blame yourself?"

"But, it *is* your fault," he said, stressing the words so calmly, so softly, and with such sureness, it instantly quieted her.

She searched his eyes for any sign of teasing. But there was no joking there. All she saw was a boyish earnestness and a man's hopeful appeal that he would be heard and believed.

Hmm. This isn't going quite the way I had planned.

"My fault, huh? Ohhh-kay. Care to explain that?" she said more harshly than necessary. But only because she was trying to keep her defenses up. Only because she could already feel her heart giving way to that look in his eyes, yielding to him . . . yearning for things to be right between them.

"Molly, I've, uh . . ." He raked his fingers through his hair, pushing it away from his forehead, revealing his serious gaze. "I've spent a lot of years doing everything I wanted to do. Just me, living spontaneously, without any regard for anyone else really. Not that I went about intentionally hurting anyone, of course." He put up a hand, she assumed to stop her from having any thoughts of that nature.

"But it was all about me, which was exactly what I wanted," he admitted, leaning forward, resting his elbows on his knees. "All about *my* plans, *my* adventures, *my* crazy, spur-of-the-moment schedules," he spoke out in the direction of the lake. "No commitments. Total freedom. Experiencing the thrill of living freely—no strings attached."

"But then . . ." He looked back at her, staring into her eyes, seeming almost puzzled about the words he was about to say. "But then, I kissed you." His voice went soft with honesty, hushed with a sort of marveling at the whole thing. And for her, his admission took her breath away almost as much as their first kiss had.

Before she knew what was happening, he sat facing her, brushing a hair away from her face. His touch was so tender she yearned to cradle her head into the palm of his hand. "Do you remember?" he asked. "When I kissed you that first night?"

As if it were even possible that she could forget?

"You asked me what I was thinking," he reminded her.

She nodded. "You said 'nothing,' but I didn't think that was altogether true."

"You were right," he chuckled. "But you can't blame me for not admitting it to you. I could barely admit it to myself. When I kissed you, Molly, all I could think about is how lucky I felt to be there with you. And how much I *wanted* to be there with you—at the bloody awful Somersby County fairgrounds of all places—instead of somewhere a bit more exotic, say perhaps, Malibu or Mt. Hood."

She chuckled. "So our kiss rated better than riding a twenty-foot wave?"

"You're laughing." He smiled. "But yes. Yes, it truly did. And it was a bit unsettling for me, too, since I'd always prided myself on being Mr. Noncommittal; the daring, never-going-to-settle-down adventurer." He puffed out his chest.

"Honestly, Molly, I'm not used to making commitments. Or involving myself in other people's lives. And, well, you have to understand, it's a tad scary for me. Frightening, really." He gave her an exaggerated horrified look.

"Drew . . . believe me, it's not just scary for you. It is for me, too. But, I'm not asking you to know exactly how strong or serious your feelings are for me right now."

"But I think I do know, Molly. I think I'm starting to sort it all out and—"

She reached up with two fingers to silence his lips. "No, please. I don't want you to say anything you might regret. I'm willing to give things time. I don't expect you to know exactly how you feel right now. But I also don't expect you to lie to me until you do know."

He reached for her fingers, and took her hand into his, rubbing it gently. "Forgive me, Molly?"

"But I still need to know, Drew, what is the truth? I mean, are you staying here? Or are you going back to Boston?"

She could feel herself holding her breath, waiting for his answer. How badly she wished he'd stay. She cared for him so much, and more than anything hoped to have more time with him.

"The absolute truth is, I never wanted to go to Boston, Molly. I told my parents I would go just to help them out. But my heart simply isn't in it. At this point, I'm thinking they'll understand. At least I hope Mum will . . ." his voice trailed off. "Right now, I'd like to spend more time in Somersby with you," he squeezed her hand, "if you'll have me."

Relieved by his words, she gazed into his face, studying him. "Were you ever a Boy Scout?"

"Pardon me?" He blinked.

"Were you a Cub Scout? Boy Scout? Eagle Scout? Whatever? Do you have some kind of Boy Scout honor thing you can swear to tell the truth by?"

He chuckled. "No, I was never in the Boy Scouts."

"Really?"

"Well, just for a week." He shrugged a shoulder. "But that hardly counts, does it? I got kicked out for chasing down a Girl Scout and kissing her. Evidently it wasn't a requirement for any of the badges we were supposed to earn." He grinned impishly at the memory. "Had to turn in my neckerchief. Sorry to say that's all I recall of that particular experience."

Oh, she should have known! She was in trouble with this one. Big, big trouble.

"But, Molly," he rushed to say, "I can swear by my heart that my feelings for you are very real and very strong. In fact, I'll swear on my mother's name that I will never lie to you again. Ever."

She had seen the love and respect he'd shown for his mother. That was an honor code she knew would hold true, wasn't it?

"All right." She raised her chin at him. "We can try it again," she nodded, and his eyes lit up. "Under one condition," she added.

His eyes dimmed a bit. He looked at her warily. "Yes?"

"You need to kiss me . . ." she mewed a soft invitation. "So we can 'kiss and make up.' "

"Ah . . ." he sighed.

Instantly, a glint of amusement brightened his eyes. His lips curled into the self-assured smile he'd been missing all night, the taunting smile she was so accustomed to. "That would be my pleasure, Molly Katz," he said, his finger tilting her chin up to him. "Undoubtedly very much my pleasure," he repeated as he lowered his head, his soft lips seeking hers.

Chapter Ten

"What's this?" Molly wiped her flour-coated hands on her Corner Coffee Café embroidered apron before taking the small white bag Drew held out to her.

"Just a bit of lunch. You do recall the concept, don't you?"

Though his words teased, the warmth in his gaze, the thoughtfulness of his gesture hinted at how much he cared. "Remember? Lunch? Something that occurs throughout the rest of the universe about midday or so? You take a break from work. Pick out a nice place to sit. Say like there, perhaps?" He pointed to an antique church pew adorned with floral cushions near the café's side window. "Then you eat something tasty. I'm hoping you like club sandwiches?"

He leaned in toward her as he spoke, his closeness overwhelming her. Reviving every tingling feeling she'd felt last night. Making her recall how completely comfortable she'd felt as they sat on the bench after they'd kissed and made up. How their moments together seemed so special, the moonlight hanging over them like a spotlight, singling them out, highlighting the feelings they shared.

It had been so hard to say good night to him. So hard that when they finally did part and she slipped under her bedcovers, she wanted nothing more than to fall asleep quickly so she could rush through the remainder of the night and wake up to see him again. And yet sleep had eluded her for hours as her mind replayed his sweet words, his loving gaze, his tender touch, over and over again.

When morning did come, she tried to make a conscious effort not to keep staring at the clock, tried not to wonder how much longer it would be till she saw him again, the minutes passing by painfully slowly.

Then before she knew it, he was there, like an apparition standing in her café, his masculine presence filling every nook and cranny of her coffee shop . . . and, of course, her heart.

Her breathing all but stopped at the sight of him. Her stomach fluttered with a million butterflies. She could feel her mouth gape open, and her heart beat a crazy rhythm all its own.

And after all that, after all of those feelings rushing through me for the past twelve hours or so, he's asking me what? Something about sandwiches?

"I—I do," she stammered, trying to concentrate on his question, her answer. "I do like club sandwiches."

"Good. I'd hoped it was a harmless choice." He

smiled. "I thought it might be good for you to take time to eat, replenish your body." His eyes danced over her with appreciation, leaving her slightly flushed. "And time to talk with an Englishman who is very fond of you and, honestly, couldn't wait till tonight to see you."

She laughed, tickled by his candidness. He seemed to be feeling the same way too.

With her free hand, she patted self-consciously at stray strands of hair, hoping—but doubting—that she looked as pretty as he always made her feel.

"Have you had much of a Sunday crowd?"

"Nothing I couldn't handle." She smiled. "Actually, I've spent most of my time this morning making extra dough and freezing it. Planning ahead, you know?"

"Sounds good. But you really should rest some too, Wonder Woman. You'll wear yourself out. Won't have the energy to work your lips into a decent pucker."

"Oh. So that's what you're really worried about," she laughed.

"Seriously, Molly, do you have a moment to sit down?"

Lifting the bag in the air, she grinned. "How can I resist?"

Making their way over to the window seat, she unwrapped the sandwich and took a few bites, noticing how pleased he seemed with himself. Because he'd gotten her to relax? Because of something else?

"Drew, really, thank you. This is such a treat. Sometimes I get so busy I don't even remember to eat during the day. And rarely do I sit to do it. And even more rarely with such good company." She offered him one of her sweetest smiles.

"You left out good-looking company. And witty too."

"Gosh, I did?" she chuckled, loving his sense of humor. "I didn't mean to."

"Well, as long as you didn't mean to." He watched her take another bite of sandwich before adding, "There's a pickle and chips in there too, if you'd like."

"Oh?" She dug through the bag. "Thank you."

Normally, she wouldn't have indulged in a pickle or chips. A sandwich was more than enough. But he looked so proud of himself that she took the extra items from the bag and tore open the bag of chips, deciding not to think about calories or fat content, or anything else for that matter—except him.

"You know, I was thinking . . ." She paused with chip in hand. "I've been pretty tired lately. Dragging actually. Just so much work, you know? And I know it's made me cranky. Maybe . . . maybe I overreacted last night."

"Overreacted? You mean because you were heaving rocks into the lake, trying to maim those poor innocent ducks, all because you were mad at me?"

"I wasn't trying to maim any ducks." She giggled, jabbing him in the shoulder playfully with her sandwich-free hand.

Before she knew it, he reached for her fist, holding his hand over hers. His tender touch gushed over her. Her fist relaxed and each of their open hands sought the others. Clasping tightly, lovingly, all the hours that had separated them since they'd seen each other last night seemed to dissipate. They were back in the moment where they had left off . . . connected again.

"I'm teasing, Molly. True, the ducks didn't deserve your wrath, but I certainly did. But again, I did nothing with the intent of hurting anyone and I—" he started to apologize.

"Drew, it's okay." She squeezed his fingers. "We talked about all of this last night."

"Yes, and speaking of last night . . ." He let go of her hand, rubbing his palms together in a way that seemed serious. Molly set the sandwich down on its wrapper, suddenly not very hungry. "Mum was still up when I got back to Blake's," he told her. "We had the chance to chat."

She wanted to respond, but was far too nervous to ask how that conversation went. The only reply she could manage was raising her eyebrows.

"I told her I had a change of plans. I told her I've decided to stay in Somersby."

"You did?" She almost gulped out loud.

He nodded. "Yes, I did."

"And . . . how did that go?"

"Surprisingly well, actually. While I thought perhaps she'd be somewhat upset, instead she hugged my neck and told me how happy she was with my decision."

He threw his arms up in the air looking totally baffled, but pleased with the outcome of the midnight talk. "It seems after all the stress and anxiety I've been putting myself through . . . and you as well . . . I have the peculiar feeling she doesn't care where I settle down, as long as I do."

"You're kidding?" She let out a sigh of relief. "Wow, women!" She rolled her eyes. "Who can figure us out, huh?"

"Not I!" He smiled down at her. "But I want you to know, I'm happy to keep trying," he added, his gaze so intent, he seemed to be kissing her, caressing her with his eyes.

She hated tearing herself away from his gaze. Didn't want to, not in the least. The feeling was so incredibly wonderful, creating an excited shiver that went all the way from her cheeks right down to her toes. But the feeling was also so intimate. And, well, what if—what if a customer came in? Surely, they'd notice it too. Of course, she didn't want to shoo him out of the café either. She wanted him to stay longer and . . .

"You could try baking with me," she said, plucking the silly suggestion out of thin air.

"Baking?" His head reared back on his shoulders. "Hmm. That wasn't exactly first on my list of things I'd like to do with you."

The alluring Dawson half-smile appeared in all its glory. She worked hard to ignore its appeal, but it wasn't that easy.

"You said your brother likes to cook." She shrugged. "So I just thought . . ."

She knew hinting at any sort of sibling rivalry would do the trick. Drew inhaled deeply, puffing out his chest. "True, true. I suppose if Blake is man enough to take on the task of cooking, I'm more than man enough to try my hand at baking." He flexed his arms in a comical way, but the sinewy ripple of muscles that appeared left her seriously speechless.

"I suppose clean hands would be a prerequisite for this baking chore?" he asked, standing up, and glancing around.

She laughed. "In my kitchen it is."

"And the loo would be where?"

"Down at the end of that hallway." She pointed to the right.

He stood up and started walking in that direction, then turned back to look at her. "This isn't a trick, is it?" he teased, smiling at her irresistibly. "You will be here when I return?"

"I'm not going anywhere."

"Good." He smiled satisfactorily. "Neither am I."

"You're one lucky bloke, I'll give you that," Drew said to his reflection in the restroom mirror as he worked his hands into a soapy lather.

Yes, he really was fortunate to have found someone like Molly. He'd met many, many girls in his travels, but she was truly one in a million. Beautiful. Bright. Independent. Vivacious. She had a way of making him feel like life was something even greater than he'd ever imagined.

Yes, he nodded to himself in the mirror, *you are one lucky fellow indeed.*

And quite lucky she's still talking to you too. His conscience took a stab at him.

I beg your pardon? His hands stopped rubbing, warm water flowing over them.

You heard me. You're lucky she's talking to you after the fib you told her.

I didn't fib. I just didn't . . . fill in all the blanks.

Uh-huh. Whatever.

Besides, everything is fine between us now. We talked last night. I explained everything. I was completely honest.

Com-plete-ly?

Well, now . . . if you're talking about the coffee thing . . .

Hmmph. I'm only talking about it because you never seem to.

You're very impatient, you know that? He squinted into the mirror, half expecting someone else to be looking back at him.

And you're quite the wimp.

Hey, I'm getting a chance to be in the kitchen today. That's a good thing, isn't it? She teaches me a little baking. In no time I'll be teaching her how to make coffee. Sounds like the perfect situation.

Rinsing his hands thoroughly, he turned off the faucet. But that didn't turn off the voice in his head.

Just don't blow it.

Blow it? He looked into the mirror, his hands still dripping in front of him. *I'm hardly some kind of monstrous creature, some idiotic fool.*

Grabbing a wad of paper towels, he dried his hands and then stepped back, checking out his reflection. *In fact, I'm a decent bloke as blokes go. And not a terribly bad looking fellow either,* he commended himself.

Tossing the towels in the wastebasket, he leaned in

closer, baring his teeth in the mirror. Clean. Straight. Decently white and bright. Yes, the teeth were fine. And the hair. Not to worry. So far, so good. He still had plenty. And his eyes. Hmm. He inched even nearer to the mirror to get a better look.

His eyes looked differently to him somehow. Turning his head back and forth, he searched for any signs of wrinkles. But no. All clear in that department. So it wasn't that.

But then what was it? His eyes narrowed in on themselves, trying to discern the change. And then he realized it. It wasn't that his eyes looked different exactly. It was more like he was seeing himself differently.

The wild-at-heart, daring look that had always been uniquely his wasn't as prevalent anymore. Instead, his eyes looked more focused.

Interesting. He blinked.

He wasn't sure what it all meant at the moment. But he had a feeling it had to do with the green-eyed beauty in the next room. The one with hair the color of a golden sunset and skin so soft and sweet-smelling he could barely keep his hands from touching it. That very special lady on the other side of the door who was waiting to teach him more about her world . . . and more about himself.

"What kind of enterprise do you think I'm running? A non-profit organization?"

As Drew stepped out of the restroom, he was surprised to hear a man's voice booming in the café. But the man wasn't just loud; his tone was obnoxious and condescending too. So arrogant it made the hairs on Drew's arms stand up on end and his hands involuntarily draw up into fists.

"I didn't want to start the work week without stopping by. You only have three more weeks," the man warned Molly, who was standing behind the café counter looking too shocked to reply. "Three weeks to pay for the partial rent you owe, plus the late fee, and September's rent as well. That was our deal. Then your time is up. Your stab at running a successful business is over. And your charming little café will be all mine."

The man's back was turned to Drew. But the Englishman watched as the ogre ran his hand over the smooth oak tabletops, looking around, taking in the details, surveying the place as if it was already his.

Just seeing this character lay a finger on one of Molly's tabletops in such a haughty, proprietary way made Drew's blood boil. And though Drew knew it'd be unfair to come up from behind and pounce on this pompous creep, it was exactly what he wanted to do. And about all he could do to restrain himself.

"Too bad," the snooty-looking man told Molly. "I'm sure it took a lot of work to get the place looking this way. But really, you've had plenty of chances. As we discussed, this is your last. Then it will be time for the amateurs to move aside, and for the professionals to take over."

That did it! Nobody came in here and talked to Molly like that. Even if the guy was wearing expensive-looking leather loafers and a Brooks Brothers sport coat. Even if it was ninety degrees outside and this insolent jerk appeared as cool and icy as the arctic tundra.

Drew charged into the room, his fists clenched tightly. "Mister, I don't know who you are, but you've got a lot of nerve talking to Molly—or any other woman for that matter—like that. Apologize or—"

"Apologize?" The man swung around to face Drew. "Apologize or what? What are you going to do? Hurt me?"

"Honestly?" A muscle quivered in Drew's jaw as he narrowed his eyes on the man. "It has crossed my mind a few hundred times in the past thirty seconds."

"Drew, please," Molly pleaded, glancing anxiously between the two men. "Don't."

"Don't what?" Drew asked her, keeping his eyes peeled on the intruder. "You'd better be more specific, Molly, because it's all I can do to keep my hands from coming in contact with his face."

Flipping back the sides of his sport coat, the man put his hands on his hips and sneered. "Apparently you don't understand *who* I am."

"Apparently," Drew mocked him, "you don't understand that I couldn't care less *who* you are. *What* you are is rude and distasteful."

"Drew!" Molly tried to assuage the situation once more. "He's my landlord, Prescott Sterling."

"The fourth," Sterling added self-importantly.

"Ah, well," Drew replied sarcastically. "We all can't be the first in everything now, can we?"

Visibly irritated by the comment, Sterling turned to Molly. "Who is this hulk of masculine stupid-tude?"

"Uh, Drew," she told him. "Drew Dawson."

"Dawson?" The name seemed to shock Sterling into silence at first. But he composed himself quickly, looking down his nose at Drew. "I should've known," he said, mild disgust in his voice.

"Clearly, this is a waste of my time. None of this matters," Sterling told them both as he edged toward the door of the café. "Three more weeks, Miss Katz. That's all you have." He shrugged indifferently. "I hope you've enjoyed your short stint as a café owner."

"Thanks a lot, Drew," Molly told him after Sterling left. But by the contempt in her tone, he knew she didn't mean it. He could hardly believe it.

"Are you quite serious? After the way he spoke to you? You're angry? *At me?*"

"You *are* the one who practically attacked him," she scolded.

"Well, he shouldn't have spoken to you like that. Besides, I was only trying to help."

"Yeah. You and every other guy who thinks I'm a helpless, defenseless female."

"I beg your pardon." He couldn't believe she was saying that. "You truly think I'm like every other guy?"

"Yes!" she answered decisively. "No." She shook her head. "Actually, I don't know what to think." She looked frustrated. "All I know is that ever since you've come to Somersby, my life has been a mess!"

"A mess?" Was she serious? "And somehow that has to do with me?"

"Well, you're the one coming in here, distracting me.

Lying to me. Getting me all confused. All I'm trying to do is work hard and run my business."

"But your business has nothing to do with me. With us."

"You're right. But your being around . . . I don't know . . . everything's been so topsy-turvy lately. It's just not helping."

"But I can help, Molly. Truly I can," he pleaded. "In fact . . . seriously, Molly, there's one very, very simple thing that could turn your café around in a flash." He snapped his fingers.

At that, she came out from behind the counter. Placing her hands on her hips, she looked like she was considering his words, making him think things were going to be all right. "Oh, yeah? One very, very simple thing, huh?"

"Well, yes . . ." He started to tell her, but she opened her mouth before he could speak.

"Well, if it's so very, very simple," she snapped at him, flinging her arms in the air, "then why do I need you? I'm sure I can figure it out all on my own."

Chapter Eleven

"Oh my gosh, Moll, you didn't!"

Molly hated the look April gave her as they stood in the lobby of the movie theater waiting for the early show to let out. Her friend had been contentedly munching on handfuls of unsalted, butter-free popcorn till Molly delivered her news. Then April's wrist went limp, and her jaw slacked in total disbelief and dismay.

She'd been dying to tell April every last detail about what had happened between her and Drew. But no wonder she had put it off. As much as she wanted to confide in her best friend, deep down she had a feeling April might react this way.

"What?" Molly asked defensively. "Why are you looking at me that way?"

"You really said that?" April looked incredulous. "You told Drew you didn't need him?"

"Well, I . . . I didn't say it like that *exactly*."

"No? Then *exactly* how did you say it?"

"I said, 'Why do I need you? I can figure out the answer on my own.'"

"Oh, great . . ." April groaned, folding the popcorn bag closed, seeming to be finished with it and possibly Molly's follies as well.

"You know, I always hate it when you groan like that. You act like I'm ruining my life. It's like something my mother would do."

"I'm sorry, Moll, but you *are* ruining your life. You and Drew are meant for each other. You really, truly, can't see that?"

"And where did you read that? In one of your *True Romance* horoscopes? Because, newsflash—" she quipped, snapping her fingers in the air, "—I think they have the wrong couple."

She'd said the words more strongly than she meant to. It wasn't April's fault that she was an incurable romantic and a well-meaning friend. "I'm sorry, April," she quickly apologized, "but Drew humiliated me in front of Sterling, acting like I couldn't handle the jerk myself. And then he made some statement like he knew how to run my business better than I could."

She heard her words replay in her mind, and added honestly, "Not that I'm doing such a great job of it myself at the moment. But you know what I mean. Maybe he seemed like a dream come true . . . but deep down inside maybe he's just another controlling, pushy, overbearing guy. And have I ever once liked a guy who was pushy? Who tried to control me? No, not at all," she answered the question herself. "I'm not willing to lose my ability to stand on my own two feet nor do I want to be dependent on someone else for my every move. Just because this charming British guy falls into my life like a newspaper thrown on someone's porch doesn't mean I—"

"Molly!" her best friend hissed at her. "Settle!" April commanded as if speaking to her pet sheltie.

April's outburst was so out of the ordinary, it startled Molly to her core. Her mouth clamped shut instantly.

"Okay," April said, pointing a silver-ringed finger at Molly. "I'm going to say something, and please don't do anything but listen."

Molly wasn't only surprised at the way April was treating her, but a little offended too. Still, it was such unusual behavior for her easygoing friend that Molly was curious about what she had to say.

"Drew is not pushy." April jabbed the air with her finger. "Drew is not chauvinistic. And you know it. He's about as sensitive as any guy can be. He's got a good sense of humor. He's interesting. And heaven knows he's great to look at."

At the mention of Drew's physical attributes, Molly and April nodded at each other in total agreement.

"And," April continued on, "the best part is—he adores you."

"Well, I don't know about th—"

"Shhhh," April hissed again, so harshly that Molly flinched. "He does. Trust me. But the point is, Moll, he isn't really the problem. If you want to know the

truth . . . you do want to know the truth, don't you?"
April's eyes narrowed in on her.

Molly nodded, too afraid to speak for fear April
would shush her again.

"Truth is, he's not the problem, Molly, you are," her
friend said matter-of-factly.

"*Me?*" she blurted out.

April nodded. "Moll, I don't know why you think
you can have things both ways, but you can't. You want
someone to be close to you, honest with you, confide in
you, and trust you with their feelings and deepest
thoughts, but then you don't want to trust them with
your feelings or your heart. You don't want their help or
to hear their thoughts as they pertain to you. It's like
you want this together thing, but then you want to be
separate." April paused long enough for Molly to digest
her words, even though she was finding them hard to
stomach.

"I don't know," April continued, wagging her head.
"It's like you're afraid if you commit yourself all the
way you'll lose yourself or something. Or maybe even
get hurt . . ." Her friend's voice softened. "But Molly,
depending on someone and having them depend on
you doesn't mean your life is over. It means you have a
new life. A life together. Ultimately, it's what makes a
family."

April had never sounded more lucid in her life.
Molly did a double-take to make sure it really was her
lighthearted, free-spirited friend talking. But, yes, it
was her, with her long shiny dark hair, large silver hoop
earrings and raisin-colored nail polish. It was truly

April, who seemed to have matured a great deal while Molly had been too busy, head buried in her own problems, to notice.

Looking around sheepishly, Molly wondered if anyone else had heard April's dissertation on how she'd been messing up her love life. But luckily, the earlier movies were letting out and everyone was coming and going, too caught up in their own conversations and lives to be concerned about hers.

As they shuffled along with the crowd, Molly considered April's assessment. "Is that something you learned from one of those magazines?" she asked weakly, realizing April was right and also thinking she needed to look into a subscription ASAP.

"No." April shook her head. "I learned that during my two years of marriage."

"Oh," Molly answered as they entered the theater and took their seats. "Then I'm really mad at you."

"Why?"

"Because you could've told me earlier," she said with a heavy sigh. "Before I ruined my life."

"Looks like April and Molly are back from the movies," Ryan commented, as Drew pulled into the couple's driveway and spotted Molly's car.

"So I notice." Drew nodded, a pain of longing tightening his gut.

"Why don't you come in, just say hi?"

"No thanks." Drew chuckled sardonically. "I think I've had enough abuse in one week to last a lifetime."

Ryan laughed.

"What?"

"That sounded kind of melodramatic and feminine, dude."

Drew considered what he'd said and how dramatically he'd said it. He laughed too. "You're right, it did."

"I can't believe you're going to let that little five-foot-five thing stand in the way of a great relationship."

"Five-foot-six," Drew corrected him, his mind drifting back to last weekend in his brother's backyard when he'd teased Molly about how comfy her five-foot-six frame felt in his arms. His hands clamped tightly around the steering wheel. "And it's slightly difficult not to. She is fifty percent of the relationship, you know."

"True. But, come on, you know women. They say things." Ryan shrugged. "It doesn't mean they always mean them."

"Oh. I think she meant what she said, all right."

"So that's it?"

"Pardon me?"

"So, you just give up that easily? This is the love of your life, man. You're not willing to fight for that?"

"Apparently, she doesn't want me to. Didn't want me to get into a row with that ridiculous Sterling bloke, even as insulting as he was. And so surly with her too."

His insides surged all over again, recalling the scene with Sterling, and then Molly. In retrospect, he should've just bopped Sterling in the nose. Either way, the result would've been the same. Molly would've thrown him out the door and out of her life. But at least he would've felt better about it in the end.

"So what do you think you're going to do?" Ryan interrupted Drew's thoughts.

Drew shrugged. "A friend of mine called from Colorado last night. Seems a group is going up to British Columbia."

"For skiing?"

Drew nodded. "Partially. A couple of them are looking for a place to live there too."

"You'd really go? Leave Somersby?"

"What's to stop me?" Drew shrugged again.

Honestly, he'd been excited to hear his old friend's voice on the phone. And the invitation couldn't have come at a better time. It was the perfect escape plan. Leave Somersby behind. Forget about all that had happened there. Go back to his old, free-bird kind of life. Plus, living in B.C. could prove to be interesting, just the twist he needed.

But then as the evening hours passed, and his mind taunted him with thoughts of Molly, the idea became less and less enticing.

But still . . . he had to go somewhere, didn't he? Was there any real reason to stay in Somersby? It would've been one thing if that had been his intent all along: to move to the small burg, build a business with his brother. But, of course, it hadn't been.

Even so, when he got there things started falling into place in a way he never expected. First with the business, and then with Molly. His initial reaction was to resist those kinds of constraints on his freedom. But after a while, without even making a conscious effort or giving it serious thought, the last place on earth he ever wanted to be had become his first choice.

But some things just aren't meant to be, he supposed. And really, life truly had been much easier before, hadn't it? Before he started caring? Before he began making commitments to people?

"I still can't believe you'd give up that easily."

Drew's jaw twitched at Ryan's words. "If you recall, I didn't. She did."

"Yeah, but . . . like I said, women get emotional. They say things they don't mean. But they're usually not so bullheaded that you can't talk to them and sort things out."

Drew looked at Ryan skeptically. "Even girls like Molly?"

"Hmm. I see your point, dude." Ryan rubbed at his chin thoughtfully. "Let me think about that one for a while, and I'll get back to you," he said indecisively, which is exactly how Drew felt.

It's weird, Molly thought, *how you never realize how much of a hole there is in your life until someone comes along to fill it. And then, when they pull up stakes, and move out of your life, it's not just a hole they leave behind anymore—it's an entire crater!*

She sunk down on a café chair, knowing it was time to close up shop for the day, but feeling too weary to even go through the routine. Maybe she'd just sit there till tomorrow morning came. Who would know the difference anyway? Who would really care?

Staring at the front door, she couldn't help but think

about the first time Drew walked into her café. Black T-shirt stretched across the fit chest she'd spilled tea on the day before. His long hair, freshly washed and shiny. His smile, curious and heart-stopping as he glanced around at her shop . . . and at her.

It felt like the world had stopped for a moment just to take time out to bring them together again after their chance meeting at the airport. Like something bigger than themselves—fate? kismet? the powers that be?—was pushing them together, working to link their hearts.

Of course, then there was the other day . . . the last time Drew walked *out* of her café. She couldn't help thinking about that either. If only she could have that day back again. She sure would do it differently. At the very least, she would've thought before speaking.

April had been right about everything, every observation she'd made. And Molly promised her that she'd call Drew and explain it all to him.

But then . . . she didn't. She couldn't. After all, she knew he'd seen her car in April and Ryan's driveway, and even though it was still early, he'd chosen not to come in. Why not? He probably never wanted to see her again. Or hear from her either for that matter. Probably thought she was more trouble than he was willing to deal with.

Besides, from the sounds of it, it seemed he had better offers on the horizon. Like skiing at Whistler and possibly even staying there for good, Ryan had told her. Evidently it wasn't too hard for him to detach himself from her or Somersby. Off to his old life so soon, he hadn't even called her to say good-bye, or to try things one last time. Not that she could really blame the guy.

So . . . She sighed heavily, glancing around at her empty shop. *This is what being independent and not wanting anyone's help gets you, huh? A love life on the rocks? And a business on the skids?*

"Great!" she said out loud and thought she heard her voice echo back. "Just great!"

She stared at the walls around her, remembering back to the day before the café opened. She'd had so much fun hanging pictures, putting together flower arrangements for the place. How completely sure she had been that all her hard work would pay off and that her business would be a success.

There must be some way. . . . she willed herself to think.

She'd thought about asking her brothers for a loan, and knew they'd give it to her in a millisecond. But then, she had to admit her self-confidence was waning at the moment. If she couldn't turn the café around . . . if she couldn't make it work again . . . well, she'd hate for them to lose their money too.

She sighed again. Drew. The café. She didn't know which loss to feel worse about. She just knew her heart ached in such an awful, painful way that she could never have imagined before.

And then . . . there seemed to be something else missing in her life lately too, she thought, glancing around the café.

Oh, yes! Mr. Mulligan. When was the last time he'd stopped by? Two days ago? Three? Was this the week he was supposed to go visit his sister in Illinois? But, no. Didn't he say that was planned for late September, beginning of October?

Obviously she hadn't been doing such a great job keeping her life together lately. It stood to reason she hadn't been keeping track of his either.

"I just hope he's okay!" she whispered to herself, as she wearily pulled her tired body out of the chair. *I don't think I could stand anything else going wrong right now.*

She started back to the kitchen area to make sure all the ovens were turned off when the bell over the café door sounded.

Every time she'd heard that bell the last few days, her heart stopped. She wished so badly she could turn around, look up, and see Drew walking back into her life with his strong, open arms . . . and tantalizing kisses . . . and sweet sense of humor. . . . She missed him so much she doubted if her heart would ever feel anything but empty again. She'd run to him and tell him over and over again how sorry she was. Tell him over and over again how much she loved him.

But once again her wishes didn't come true. There was a fit-looking man standing in her café, but it definitely wasn't Drew.

"Have any muffins left for sale?" he asked.

Molly pointed to the trays in the case, and the basket of muffins sitting on top of the counter. "Plenty. I'll even sell them for half price. I was just about to close anyway."

"I appreciate it, but you don't have to. I don't mind

paying full price for these muffins. It seems only fair since we usually get them for free anyway."

"Free? From where?"

"From here." He looked at her curiously. "From Stew."

"Stew?" She didn't recall anyone named Stew who frequented the café.

"Actually his name is Aidan," the man explained. "Mulligan. At the station we call him Stew as in Mulligan's stew."

"Oh!" She chuckled. "You're a friend of Mr. Mulligan's from the fire house?"

The man nodded. "But he hasn't been in for a few days, and we've been jonesing for some Corner Coffee Café muffins. I thought I'd give the guys on the night shift a treat and grab some on my way in."

"Mr. Mulligan hasn't been by to see you either?" A feeling of alarm tensed her nerves.

The man shook his head. "How about you?"

She shook her head in return. "That makes me feel awful. I guess I've been so caught up in my own drama this week, I didn't even stop to realize how long it'd been since I'd seen him."

"That's easy to do." The firefighter shrugged forgivingly.

"I suppose," she said, not feeling too good about herself. "I'll check on him before I go home tonight," she promised.

"If there's any problem, you know where to find us. Tell him his buddies at the station miss him." The fireman reached into his jeans for his wallet. "He needs to get in to see us, muffins or no muffins. Although trust me," he said, smiling, leaning over the counter to pay, "your muffins have to be the best in town. We're sure glad to have 'em whenever we can get 'em," he winked.

Chapter Twelve

Molly knocked on the door of Mr. Mulligan's ranch-style home several times, but still there was no answer. Peeking in the windows, she tried to see if he was there, if any lights were on. But it was still fairly light outside. He may not have needed them on yet. The only clue that Mr. Mulligan might be inside was the droning sound of a television.

Anxiety mounting by the second, she stood on her elderly friend's front porch wondering what to do.

Was she overreacting? Maybe he'd just taken a walk around the block and left the TV on while he was out. But then again, no one had seen him for days. Maybe he'd fallen and hit his head and was lying inside unconscious. Her stomach tightened into a sickly knot at the thought.

What on earth should she do? Her mind raced. Should she break a window? Call his buddies at the fire station?

Something drew her eyes to a small terra-cotta pot of pink geraniums on the corner of the porch. Something else made her bend over and pick up the pot. Sure enough, lying underneath was a gold key shining back at her.

Using it to open Mr. Mulligan's door, she prepared herself to be greeted by air conditioning. But instead, the air inside his house felt even warmer than the evening air outside. Stale and sickly smelling, it instantly caused panic to well up inside her.

"Please, God," she uttered in a hushed voice, "please let him be all right."

Strangely, an image of Drew flitted across her mind at that moment. How she wished he was here with her now. She wouldn't have turned down his help this time. She would have appreciated it, would have been grateful for the security of having him by her side.

"Mr. Mulligan?" she called out in the semi-light living room.

There was still no answer, so she moved cautiously through the house. For some reason, maybe just because Mr. Mulligan was male, she'd expected to look in on a messy kitchen with dishes piled up everywhere. But it didn't look like that at all. Instead it appeared ominously neat and tidy, with only a few items out of place: a can opener left lying on the counter, a silver pot sitting empty on the stove. It looked as if someone had started to cook something, but had to stop in mid-task, like they just couldn't manage to finish.

"Mr. Mulligan!" She heard the quiver in her voice.

Shadows played games on her eyes as she crept

down the ranch's hallway, feeling hesitant and scared. Frightened at what she might find, she poked her head into each room cautiously until she came to the largest bedroom at the end of the hall. The television was the only sound that greeted her. On the bed, the form of a person half-sitting, half-lying was silent.

No, God, no! she cried to herself, staring at Mr. Mulligan's sweet, crinkled face, the covers tucked up over his chest.

Holding her breath, she moved closer to the bed, her legs almost too weak to get her there.

Was he breathing? She tried to fix her eyes on the blankets pulled up over him.

Was his chest rising and falling? It was so hard to tell in the dimming light of the room and with the mound of blankets.

"Mr. Mulligan?"

She wanted to shake him, but her arms felt like lead, too heavy to move.

"Mr. Mulligan!" she said more sternly, a stray tear trickling down her cheek.

"Mmmm . . . enn?"

At first, Molly didn't think she'd really heard Mr. Mulligan's voice. The sound was soft as a whisper . . . a hoarse, weak groan.

She found the remote and turned down the sound on the TV. Then she leaned nearer to her friend, speaking his name again. This time she was sure he answered.

"Mary Ellen?" His eyes still closed, the words came out in a croaky mumble.

Molly's heart wrenched, hearing Mr. Mulligan say his deceased wife's name.

"It's me, Mr. Mulligan," she told him, hating to disappoint him, "Molly."

His brows furrowed together.

"Molly. From the café. Corner Coffee Café," she said.

But he didn't show any signs of recognizing her name.

"Blueberry muffins?" she tried. "You like my blueberry muffins."

At that, his eyebrows arched, the right side of his mouth turned slightly upward, and the relief she felt was overwhelming. Still, she knew neither of them was out of the woods yet. She needed to get a better look at him to fully assess the situation, and the room was growing dimmer by the minute.

"I'm going to turn on a lamp, Mr. Mulligan, so keep your eyes closed if you'd like," she told him.

Clicking on the lamp, she nearly gasped out loud. Clearly, whatever illness Mr. Mulligan was suffering from, it was certainly taking a toll on his body. Cracked lips. Sunken cheeks. Wizened skin and gray whiskers shooting out around his chin and jawline. He looked like he had aged ten years in the past week. Plus, his frame seemed shrunken from the friend she knew. And she could tell from the way his breathing came in shallow gasps he was still in much discomfort.

Reaching out, she felt his forehead. It was hot to her touch. The relief she'd been feeling was replaced by fright and anxiety all over again.

"Mr. Mulligan, do you know how long you've been sick?"

With visible effort, he opened his eyes halfway. "Rain," he answered.

Rain? Did he mean since it had rained? That had been four days ago. Panic tightened her throat till it felt nearly closed.

"Are you in pain?" she managed to ask.

He shook his head, ruling out appendicitis or an inflamed gallbladder or something, she assumed. Did that mean it was the summer flu that had been going around? If so, how dehydrated was he? And at his age, how much could his system tolerate?

"We need to get you to a hospital, Mr. Mulligan. Someone needs to have a look at you."

She had barely gotten the words out of her mouth, when his hand reached for her, clamping over her arm.

He shook his head again, this time quite vehemently. His eyes looked as frightened as a child's. And then she remembered . . . recalled the story he had told her one day about all he had gone through with his wife's illness. About how much he hated hospitals because people went into them and never came out. People died in them just like his bride of fifty-one years had.

"Then you're going to have to follow my instructions, Mr. Mulligan."

His eyes had already started to close, but his lip curled up slightly again at the sound of her words.

"I'm going to get some Tylenol® and a huge glass of water for you to drink. We need to get your fever down."

He didn't seem to protest, so she padded into the kitchen in search of a fever reducer and some water.

Seeing the empty pot on the stove, she wondered about the last time he'd eaten.

Well, the main thing is to start getting the fever down and to hydrate him, she thought to herself. She'd make some soup for him in a little bit.

If she couldn't get the fever down, she realized she really would have to do something more drastic. Seek professional help, whether her friend liked it or not.

Or call Drew . . .

Unable to stop herself, her thoughts kept turning back to him. But it was silly really. What? Call him in British Columbia or wherever else he was? And he was going to do what exactly? Come running back to Somersby? Back to the place she'd personally chased him away from?

Exhausted, Molly moved a few articles of clothing from a cushioned chair in the corner of Mr. Mulligan's bedroom and settled down in it, drawing her legs up under her and a lightweight afghan over her. It was way after midnight, but she felt like perhaps she'd made some headway with her elderly friend in the past few hours.

He had slept for some time after she'd given him the Tylenol® and made him drink plenty of water. When he woke up, his forehead felt cooler than before. He was more talkative too, explaining to her how, after not being able to keep any food down for a couple of days, he'd become too weak and dizzy to even get out of bed. It lightened her heart when he agreed to try a little bit of soup. Of course, she reprimanded him the entire time he was eating about how he could've at least picked up the phone and called her for help.

His breathing seemed more even as he slept now, less labored than before. But his body still looked small and fragile under the covers. It made her think back to the day—actually the first time Mr. Mulligan and Drew met in her café. With cane in hand, Mr. Mulligan had struggled to get out of his chair and into a standing position. It was normal procedure for the older man, but Drew seemed to instinctively move closer to him, ready to catch Mr. Mulligan if he fell.

Molly remembered noticing the vast physical difference between the retired firefighter and the young British sports enthusiast. Remembered thinking how easy it would have been for Drew to hoist Mr. Mulligan over his shoulder and carry him wherever he wanted to go all day long.

Her heart cinched in pain at the memory. It was so obvious, so painfully obvious, that Drew wasn't an overbearing person. She'd known that all along. Why hadn't she allowed herself to believe it before now? He was kind and thoughtful. He wouldn't hesitate to help anyone along his way. Why, he'd even helped her with her computer problem, and all he wanted in return was . . .

Her body shook with sobs as she thought back to their first date . . . their first "adventure." He had looked so cute when he came to pick her up, tan and fit, in his faded jeans and white button down with the sleeves rolled up. He looked a little too nice and clean to be dragging him off to the county fair.

But even in all the dust and heat, he hadn't seemed to

mind at all. Well, at least once they got past the blue ribbon pigs anyway. How she'd laughed at the faces he'd made at them. Oh, and then the mechanical bull! She'd been so frightened for him. And then so pleased with herself when she'd ridden the beast sidesaddle and Drew swung her in the air, proud as anything of her. And then, on the bench by the riverbank . . .

Oh, dear God, help me! her mind wailed as she remembered his closeness . . . his kiss . . . the way he'd looked at her . . . the way he'd taken her breath away. *Please, God, please!*

Grabbing the afghan, she pulled it up to her mouth, trying to muffle her crying. But she couldn't mute the sound of her voice in her head . . . probing, questioning. How? What? Why did she ever let him go?

"Molly?"

He'd come to get her! He was calling her name. She wanted so badly to get to him. Didn't want to miss the chance. But her body was so, so heavy. And she was so, so tired. She just . . . couldn't . . . move.

I'm here, she tried to tell him. But her words got lost somewhere . . . somehow. Where was the sound? Turn up the audio. Could he—would he—still find her? She could see him so clearly. Right . . . there. Almost next to her. Just needed his arms to carry her . . . close to him. That's all . . . his arms, his shoulder . . . and everything would be good again.

I love you, Drew. I love you, I love you. She'd say over and over again to him once he got to her, once he found her.

"Molly?"

The voice came louder, stronger. And so did the horribly hurtful, painful realization that the voice—the one calling her name—didn't belong to him.

"Wha—?" Her eyelids would barely open, so heavy and swollen as if she'd been . . . crying all night.

Her heart knotted in her chest as her eyes adjusted to the sunlight streaming into the room. And she realized she had been crying through the hours of darkness. But it hadn't changed a thing. It hadn't brought Drew back to her today.

"You don't look so good," the voice said to her and this time she recognized who it was, where she was.

"I'm okay, Mr. Mulligan," she fibbed bravely, her entire body aching along with her broken heart.

"Doesn't look like it," he told her as he sat up in bed, looking more like himself again, and a lot better than she felt. "That Tylenol® you gave me in the middle of the night did wonders for me, but you look like . . . well, you look like you need to go home."

She shook her head and realized it hurt too. "I'm going to make you some toast and maybe some oatmeal if you have any."

"No need," her friend protested. "I feel much better. I can do that myself."

"No, I'm taking care of breakfast," she said, though the thought of any food sounded totally nauseating. "Then I'm checking your temperature, and after that, I'm picking up a few things at the grocery store for you."

The list of duties she'd compiled for herself suddenly made her feel completely weary. Especially since first on the list was to get up out of the chair, and she wondered how she'd even manage to do that.

"You need to rest, Molly girl. Or you need to be at the café."

"It's Sunday. I'm never that busy on Sundays. And I can rest after I get you settled."

"But—"

"Mr. Mulligan, please." She really didn't have the energy to argue with him. "I'm the boss here," she said with more strength than she felt, trying to keep up a strong front.

Chilled, she wrapped the afghan around her shoulders and with painstaking effort pushed herself out of the chair.

Another day without Drew. Somehow she had to get through it. Somehow she had to survive it. Would she? Somehow?

Chapter Thirteen

Drew stared numbly as Blake gathered Emma in his lap, slipping pink sandals onto her tiny feet, getting her ready to drop off at daycare before their Monday morning business appointment.

He had never really pictured himself in a paternal role before. It had seemed like something in the far distance. Something meant for someone else. Something with a big question mark attached to it, and an apathetic question mark at that.

But seeing his brother and niece together, father and daughter, made him mourn a role he suddenly realized he might never be destined for. Because now he knew what it felt like to hold a little one in your lap, to have a little one in your life. To feel them clasp on to your finger for dear life. And giggle at your silly faces . . . or gurgle your name. Now he knew in more ways than one what it felt like to have someone look at you with trust and love.

Before arriving in Somersby he thought he knew so much about the world. Why wouldn't he? He'd seen much of it, and had enjoyed much of it. But since coming to his brother's small hometown, his eyes had been opened wider. He knew a lot more now about a lot of things.

"Man, what are you waiting for?" Blake looked up from his daughter.

"What do you mean? I've been sitting here ready for the past ten minutes waiting for you."

"I mean 'what are you waiting for' as in you need to bring some closure to this thing with Molly. No disrespect, but you're a mess, bro. You fly out to British Columbia, that lasts for all of three days; you come back here, but you barely do more than sit and stare off into space. You've been moping around here for the past week," his brother recapped his whole sorry life while Emma squirmed in his lap. "Just go talk to her. Get it out of your system. And while you're at it, tell her the truth, Drewster. At least maybe her business can be saved."

Meaning that our relationship can't?

Drew sighed, his chest heavy. "I suppose it's not as if I have anything to lose, do I now?"

His brother didn't say a word, but his sorrowful, sympathetic expression was answer enough, looking as if someone—or something—had died. Drew could certainly relate. Every fiber of his being surely felt that way.

He'd been telling himself the same thing for the past couple of days, that he needed to go talk to her, tie up the loose ends once and for all. Tell her about the coffee situation, possibly give her a chance to salvage her business. He'd hate himself forever if he didn't at least do that. And Molly only had about another two weeks or so before Sterling would evict her, the rotten jerk.

So what was he waiting for?

How about more time? Maybe enough time to stop hurting? Enough time to pass so he could see her and not want her? Time to learn to love again?

Would there ever be enough time for all of that?

"You can handle the appointment by yourself?"

His brother arched his brows, and nodded with certainty. "Honestly, I think I can manage." And then he added, because Drew was sure he wanted him to consider staying in Somersby, "Although I'm hoping not to have to make a practice of it."

As Emma wiggled down from Blake's lap, his brother got up and came to his side. "Hard to believe, I know, bro, but somehow things usually work out for the best." He clapped Drew on the shoulder consolingly.

"Thanks," Drew muttered, knowing it was an age-old platitude, but also knowing he had never wanted to believe anything more in his life.

He just didn't know if he could.

Seeing Corner Coffee Café dark and all locked up, Drew's heart lurched in his chest. There was only one thing left to do—get back in the car and dash over to Molly's townhouse.

Hopefully, she hadn't done something drastic. Hopefully, she was just fine and hadn't given up and turned the café over to Sterling before the allotted time was up.

But that didn't sound like Molly. She was determined, a fighter, a scrapper; not a quitter. An independent woman. Wasn't that the reason they'd gotten to this stage with one another in the first place? Or at least one of the reasons?

The parking spaces in front of the row of townhouses were empty, except for Molly's car. This filled him with mixed emotions. On the one hand, he was relieved she was there because he wouldn't have known where else to look for her. But then again, he was worried. Apparently, all the other residents had left for work. Why hadn't she?

Pulling up alongside her car, he grabbed the keys out of the ignition and ran up to her door. Surely she was okay in there, wasn't she?

Pounding on the front door with his fist, it took him a moment to realize he was pummeling the thing like a madman. She'd have to be crazy to open the door for him. So instead he edged closer, pressing her doorbell with as much self-control as he could muster. Once. Twice.

And when there wasn't a quick answer at the door. Three times. Four. Five, for good measure.

Impatient, he started to go around to her back patio, when he thought he heard something. Leaning in to listen, he couldn't be too sure. Was that movement coming from inside?

Pressing closer, he put his ear to the door. He almost fell in when she opened it.

"Uh, hello there," he said, embarrassed, trying to regain his balance.

Standing there in her pajama pants and oversized T-shirt, she appeared totally dazed, her eyes forming tiny, squinty slits.

"Drew?" she mumbled, her mouth barely moving. "Drew . . ." She bobbed forward. "I love. . . . love . . . you . . ."

That was pretty much all the conversation they had time for before Molly swayed and her legs buckled. And then she fainted, toppling over right into his open arms.

He didn't need to be a rocket scientist or an M.D. to know that Molly was running an extremely high temperature. He could feel the heat coming off every part of her body as he carried her up the steps to her bedroom. Though he couldn't deny how good it felt to hold her in his arms again, the worry he was experiencing far outweighed the pleasure.

Amazingly she had made it down the steps in one piece, as weak as she was.

Thank God for that! He rolled his eyes heavenward.

Laying her feverish body gently down on the bed, he pulled a light sheet over her. Then for a moment, he just stared at her. He'd missed her so much over the past week. Hadn't gone a morning without waking up with her on his mind. And, though he'd tried to concentrate on other things, and tried to run to other parts of the country, he hadn't gone ten minutes without trying to sort out all that had happened between them. Not ten minutes without thinking how much he loved her.

Did she really say she loved me?

He had really, truly heard that, right? Or was he making it up?

Are you kidding? She's on fire with fever, man, his inner voice chided.

Yes, yes, I know. But perhaps it's causing a truth serum effect or something.

Or it's pure delirium! The voice scoffed again.

Whatever the case, it didn't matter. He wanted to believe she loved him more than anything. And that's what he planned to do. But now wasn't the time to think about all of that anyway. Molly was extremely ill and needed his help.

And luckily she's too sick to turn it down, he thought, as he moved outside her bedroom door, took out his cell phone and speed-dialed Sam's extension at the agency.

"Sam, I hope I'm not bothering you . . ." his voice trailed.

"Drew? Is everything all right?"

She has enough sixth sense for ten women, he thought, glad he didn't have to go through the small talk.

"Not really. I'm at Molly's place. And she's bloody burning up with fever."

"Molly's? How did—I mean, when did—oh, never mind. What can I do?"

"It's more like, what can *I* do?" he asked her. "Or what should I do? Obviously, I know I have to get some Tylenol® or something in her, but—"

"And liquids too. You can't let her dehydrate. Do you think it's from that flu? That thing is wicked. Em ran a fever for days. And if Molly's been sick to her stomach, she could be dehydrated from that too, dizzy, faint . . ."

His hand tightened around the phone. "Actually she collapsed in my arms when I first arrived here."

"Oh, no, Drew. Thank goodness you went over there. You know, there's another thing you can do to try to bring down the fever. Get a bowl of tepid water and a washcloth and just gently run it over her limbs, on her cheeks, her forehead. Sometimes that helps cool a person down."

"Tepid water, huh?"

"Not cold. And not hot."

"Got it!" He peeked into the room. Molly was in the same position he'd left her in and still dozing.

"Say the word, Drew, and I'm on my way," his thoughtful sister-in-law offered. "I can be there in ten minutes."

"I'll try this first. Believe me, if it doesn't work, you'll be the first to know. It helps just knowing you're available if I need you."

"Well, don't forget it," she stressed. "I'll be thinking of you. Call and let me know how things are going, okay?"

"Thanks, Sam. I will."

It took about ten minutes for him to scour the house and locate all the items he needed. He carried them up to Molly's bedroom on a tray he'd found in a kitchen cabinet. Clearing her nightstand, he set the tray down.

Sitting gingerly on the edge of her bed, he took a deep breath.

"Molly, you're going to have to wake up for a moment. I need to give you something for your fever, love. Okay?" he pleaded softly. "Molly?"

He didn't want to shake her awake. He could just imagine how sensitive her skin must feel with the fever coursing through it. Instead, he stroked her cheeks with the palm of his hand. They were hot to the touch and flushed, but just as soft and creamy-feeling as he'd remembered.

"Hey there, love," he said in a half-whisper. "Can you hear me? Molly?"

Well, if she wasn't responding to his voice . . .

Leaning close to her, he could feel the heat coming off her skin . . . and feel the familiar longings of his desire for her rising up inside him. Bending his head toward hers, he gently, tenderly, kissed her dry, burning forehead.

Her eyes stay closed, but her hand moved upward. Searching, touching her skin where his lips had been.

"Hey, you," he spoke quietly.

She still lay motionless, but suddenly there was movement behind her eyelids.

"I know you're in there," his hushed voice teased.

He watched and waited and finally was rewarded when she slowly opened her green gemlike eyes.

"There you are." He smiled, a slight feeling of relief washing over him.

She stared at him blankly. And he knew she wasn't

really hearing him, but all the while he talked softly to her anyway. Propping her head up with his arm, he coaxed her into taking the fever medication along with some long drinks of water and sips of a lemon-lime soda he'd brought upstairs for her. Before he knew it, she slipped off to sleep again.

Lifting the sheet lightly from her body, he wet the washcloth in the tepid water and squeezed it so it wasn't dripping. Then he gently rubbed the soft cloth up and down her bare arms, across her forehead, and held it against her cheeks. Pushing up her pajama pants slightly, he ran the damp cloth over her shins and calves, up to her knees. He thought back to the day in the airport when she'd made a remark about her sandals, and his eyes had been drawn to her lovely, tan legs. So much had passed between them since then. Who would've ever imagined that day that he—Mr. Never-Get-Involved-Adventurer—would be here now nursing her back to health? Turning his back yet another time on his past way of life, hoping for a way to mend their relationship?

Life certainly is funny that way, isn't it?

He repeated the damp washcloth process over and over till the water got too cool. Lost in the depths of her fever, Molly barely stirred under his touch. Glancing at the clock, he made a mental note when to start the process all over again. Then he watched over his spiritless Molly as she slept, thinking just how much he loved her.

So cold, so cold, she thought over and over again. She could feel the weight of blankets piled on top of her, tucked in around her, and pulled up to her chin. And yet, she still shivered and shook, feeling chilled to the bone.

Aching from head to toe, it felt like a century since she'd last slept. Her limbs heavy, paralyzed with fatigue, that's all she wanted to do—sleep. Rest. Escape. Dream.

And she had dreamed, hadn't she? That he was there . . . near her . . . close by. Never, ever going away. He'd made a promise, sealed it with his kiss, on her forehead. Just sleep and dream . . . a dream a day keeps the hurt away.

Chapter Fourteen

Molly popped open one eye and lay very still beneath the blankets.

Is that noise really someone . . .

Her other eye flung open in panic.

. . . whistling?!

Her eyes darted back and forth, surveying her surroundings. She felt like she'd been asleep for a year and had lost all her bearings. But then she spied a circular brass sconce on the wall, the one with a ring of glass votive holders that she'd sprung for from Pottery Barn. And on the dresser, the antique lamp with the beaded shade that she'd gotten at an estate sale . . . a photo of her brothers . . . and a small sterling silver jewel box. Yes, this was definitely her room, all right. But if this was her bedroom in her townhouse then how could—or rather, who could—possibly be whistling?

Too frightened to move, and barely able to breathe,

she stared at the ceiling, straining to hear more. A moment passed and then there it started again. Yes, it was definitely whistling. No doubt about it. And it was definitely getting closer.

She glanced at the nightstand for some kind of weapon, a book or something, but it had all been cleared away. The only thing left there was an empty plastic water bottle.

Sticking her arm out from the covers she grabbed it and lay still with it in her hand. It wasn't much, but if she lobbed it at the intruder's head, it might startle him—whoever he was.

As the whistle came closer and closer, her heart picked up pace, beating faster and faster. Finally, the whistler poked his head in her room.

Drew?!

"Well, hello there. You're finally awake?" As his well-toned body towered over her bed, she noticed he looked extraordinarily pleased to see her—or to see that she was awake anyhow. "Thirsty, are you?" He nodded at the empty water bottle.

"I, uh . . . oh, no," she stammered. "I'm, um . . . fine."

He was a sight for sore eyes—her sore eyes. Even with a couple of days' stubble covering his face, and some kind of faded logo T-shirt thrown on haphazardly, he still looked totally appealing to her, and every feeling of want that she'd ever had for him came bubbling to the surface. It made her feel weak all over again.

In the meantime, she could feel that her lips were dry, her hair was sticking up in all directions, and she realized how awful she must look. And then lying there holding an empty water bottle in her hand . . . well, she was probably looking pretty silly too. Self-consciously, she sat the bottle back on the nightstand.

"You've been sick for days," he told her, confirming her worst fears about her appearance. "Rather scared me," he added quietly, sweetly.

"It did?"

Though she wanted to hide her mussed head from him, she couldn't help staring at him in disbelief. Wasn't he supposed to be a million miles away from here? A gazillion miles away from her? *Is he really here?* She blinked. *This isn't just a dream?*

"You passed out in my arms the first day you were sick."

"Me? Passed out?" She sat up at the news. "I've never passed out."

"Well, you did." He confirmed with a nod. "I was extremely worried."

She could still see hints of that worry in his eyes as he spoke to her. It was so incredibly sweet that he'd taken care of her for days. And that he'd been so concerned. But really, he needn't have been. She'd been sick before; somehow she would have managed.

"For days the fever rampaged through your body," he told her. "At times, I thought you were nearly delirious the way you'd mumble on. I'd sit here and watch you, force you to take liquids and the fever reducer."

Delirious? She didn't know about that, but she did recall having endless, hazy dreams. Many of them about Drew, and now she knew why, since evidently he'd been hovering over her for days. Hopefully, she hadn't babbled on about her innermost feelings for him too.

"I even cooled you down," Drew continued, clueless as to what she was thinking, "wiping your sweaty, feverish limbs with a damp washcloth."

Sweaty? The word brought her thoughts to a halt. Sweaty, as in not smelling too fragrant? No lip gloss? Or mascara? Or even a brush run through her hair?

Uh-oh. She needed to get him out of the room so she could get up and pull her hair into a ponytail or something. Anything to make her feel more presentable.

"I changed my mind," she told him. "I am thirsty."

"Really? Great." He clapped his hands together. "What would you like? Soda? Water? Juice? Iced tea? A sports drink perhaps?"

Odd. She had all that in her refrigerator?

"I ran to the grocery store and stocked up," he explained to her, making her heart melt even more. *He went to the grocery store for me?*

But then her mind jolted. She had gone to the supermarket recently, too, hadn't she? She'd gotten water, and soup, and *men's deodorant? Oh, my gosh! Mr. Mulligan!*

Jerking off the covers, she bolted out of bed.

"Whoa, woman!" Drew's head jerked back. "Where do you think you're going so fast?"

"Mr. Mulligan," she said frantically. "I've got to get over there."

"Not on your life."

Laying his strong hands on her shoulders, Drew worked to steady her. She didn't quite have her sea legs and could feel her knees wobbling under her.

"But he's sick," she protested.

"No, *you're* sick." Drew looked her straight in the eyes. "Mr. Mulligan is fine now. He called on Tuesday to thank you for nursing him back to health."

"Tuesday!" Her stomach growled along with her voice. "What day is it now?"

"Molly, I think you'd better sit down. Seriously. You're looking somewhat peaked again."

Leading her over to the bed, Drew gently pushed on her shoulders till she acquiesced and sat on the edge of the mattress. "So . . . what day is it?" she asked softly.

"Uh . . ." Drew paused. "It's Thursday."

"Thursday?" she shrieked and jumped up once more. But a stabbing pain shot across her forehead, knocking her back down again. She tried to rub the pain away. "I've got to get to the café," she murmured.

Drew knelt down in front of her, tucking her mussed hair behind her ears. Touching her forehead soothingly, he spoke to her gently. "You can go tomorrow, I promise. But right now, you need to get some food in you. That will stop your knees from buckling and your head from aching."

Though she didn't want to believe it, she knew he was right. And though she didn't want to admit it, his cool hand did feel good on her forehead. But letting herself yield to his touch . . . or to the idea that they could be together again . . . would be foolish. She'd severed the love that had bound them weeks ago. Just because Drew was here now didn't mean he'd forgotten that. It just meant he was a nice guy and . . .

"How did you even—I mean, why were you at my house?" She crinkled her nose at him.

"Hmm?" He got up from his knees and started fussing with the pillows, fluffing them. "What did you say you wanted to drink?"

"Drew!" She giggled. "I asked you a question."

"And I asked you one." He smiled. "You know, you've been such a good, compliant patient, up until now, that is . . ." his voice trailed.

"How could I not be?" she squealed. "I was sleeping off a fever, according to you."

"Exactly!" He laughed out loud. "Don't ruin your fine record now that you're awake and feeling better."

She giggled along with him, and when their laughter subsided she looked at him and sighed. "I'm embarrassed you did all this for me, Drew. I mean, I've been sick before, but I've never, ever needed anyone to actually take care of me."

"Oh, I know. You're a regular one-girl team, you are."

His snide comment wasn't lost on her. Still, she tried to act like she didn't notice, tried not to think back to their last conversation in the café. "Thank you. It was really sweet of you."

He shrugged off her gratitude. "Honestly, I had help at times. April stopped in and relieved me. Sam came by too."

"But still . . ."

"Not a problem," he said, glancing at his watch as if gauging how much more time he could spare with her. "Right now, I'm going to warm up the chicken noodle soup that Blake made for you. But not to worry," he snickered, "I've tested it first. Didn't want you to become ill all over again."

"That's considerate of you." She smiled. "I didn't think Blake knew how to make anything other than chili."

"Apparently he does now. When he learned how sick you were, he dug through some soup recipes till he found one he thought he could master."

"Aw, that's so sweet. Please thank him for me. You Dawson brothers are regular miracle workers."

"Yes, well . . ." He glanced at his watch again. "Was that a juice or a sports drink?"

She knew he needed to leave. And she knew he'd already done so much. So she tried to not to think about what had been—and what might have been—and attempted to focus on the moments they had left together.

A shower had never felt so good in her life. Molly wanted to let the hot water run over her body forever. And shampoo, what a luxury! She scrubbed over every inch of her scalp twice to make sure it was squeaky clean.

After showering, drying her hair, and putting on a loose pair of cotton capris and a V-neck T-shirt, she spent some time going through the mail that had piled up and sorting through laundry she hadn't gotten to over the weekend.

By that time, her energy waned and she plopped down on the couch in her family room to rest. And wait.

When Drew left that morning, he said he'd stop by

again to check on her. She had started to protest, but he pretty much turned a deaf ear on her.

In truth, she never wanted him to leave at all. And in reality, it seemed as if he hadn't. A shirt of his still lay over one of the kitchen chairs; a pair of his sunglasses sat on a family room table. And besides those real live remembrances of him, there were the intangible ones too, like his scent, pleasantly surprising her when she walked into a room, and his presence, still lingering all around her.

She closed her eyes, rehashing their encounter that morning. Drew's light touches, his warm smile and concern, even his teasing, all seemed so loving, making her think they might be able to salvage the relationship they had begun before. But then the way he kept checking his watch, and evading her questions—well, all of that didn't seem to jive and drained the hope right out of her.

And why did I make that remark about never, ever needing anyone's help to get better? She groaned inwardly. *Will I ever learn?*

Though deep down, she knew the answer. As much as she loved Drew being there, she couldn't stand the idea of him thinking she couldn't manage on her own. And why? Why did that matter so much?

Sitting there mentally berating herself, the doorbell rang and hope sprang her to life again. Drew was back already? He wanted to make it work too?

Jumping up from the couch, she bolted to the front door, her pulse racing. Flinging the door open, her head swam. She had definitely popped up from the sofa way too quickly. Dizzy, she held onto the door for support.

"Oh . . . Mr. Mulligan." She tried not to sound disappointed, but apparently it didn't work.

"I know. You were expecting the other guy. The young, handsome one. But you're stuck with me. In fact, he can't make it, and he's the one who sent me here."

He walked in the door right past her, sans invitation. Hobbling into the family room with his cane, he took a moment to get situated on the couch.

"How are you feeling?" she asked him, sitting in a chair opposite him.

"Couldn't be better, thanks. Or I should say thanks to you." He grinned. "But I feel awful about getting you sick, Molly girl. Sorry about that." He rubbed his chin shyly.

"Oh, no, it wasn't you, I'm sure. It doesn't work that fast. I've just been tired and rundown for a while. And I've been around people with the flu. One way or another, I would've caught it regardless."

"Wicked thing, that flu," he cackled.

"Apparently. I guess I've been out of it for days."

"But that Drew boy of yours, he took good care of you."

She shifted uneasily in her seat, not sure which words made her feel more uncomfortable, "*boy of yours*" or "*took care of you.*"

"Good guy," Mr. Mulligan added. "Even if he is of British descent," he said wryly.

"Great guy, yes." So great, she kept wishing she could get him off her mind.

Silence hung between them for a moment till Mr. Mulligan spoke up again. "You and I are a lot alike, you know that, Molly girl?"

"You mean good-looking and fun to be around?" she teased.

"Yes, there's that." He chuckled. "But I was thinking more along the lines that we're both stubborn and want to do things ourselves, our way." Laying his cane across his lap, he took a long breath before continuing. "I know I've told you before, but Mary Ellen used to fuss over me like I was her most prized possession." A fond smile lit up his face momentarily, till a shadow of despair quickly chased it away.

"But what did I do? Did I thank her? Appreciate her? No, I didn't. I'd scoff at her, shoo her away. All because I was a grown man—a firefighter for St. Pat's sake. Never wanted anyone to think I couldn't take care of myself." He shook his head dismally.

"Now I wonder . . . what was I thinking?" he said, looking at her with such torment in his eyes, it broke her heart. "In my heart of hearts," he admitted to her, "I loved being loved that way by my wife. She was the sweetheart of my life." His voice cracked. "I don't know why I ever pushed her away. All she wanted to do was show her love for me and now . . . now I wish . . . I'd give anything if she were here to fuss over me and love me that way again. But it's too late for me, Molly girl. Far too late."

He stared at her and she could tell his eyes were misting up the same as hers.

"Do you . . ." she faltered. "Do you think it's too late for me?" she asked quietly, almost afraid to hear one of his typically blunt answers.

Shaking his head, he told her, "Not from what I've seen. After what I saw him do for you this past week, well . . ." He shrugged. "I'm not a mind reader, but I read people fairly well."

"Oh, Mr. Mulligan, I love him so much." Her hands tightened into fists. "But it's so hard to change, to let go."

"Hmmph," he replied. "You want to know hard? Hard is when they're gone for good. Then you'd give anything to change."

Mr. Mulligan had often said many things she didn't want to hear. But this time she knew he'd said something she needed to listen to. He was so right, and she'd been so stubborn. And seeing him sitting there looking completely forlorn touched her deeply. She moved over to the couch and put her hand over his.

"Mr. Mulligan, thank you. I know it's hard to share something like that." She patted his hand. "And I want you to know—I mean, I know it's not the same thing as having your wife here, but you do have people close by who care about you and want to fuss over you. Like me. And your sister. And Drew would do anything for you too. And the guys at the firehouse. Did I tell you? When you were sick, one of the guys came to the café and was really concerned about you."

Seeing Mr. Mulligan's eyes suddenly brighten, she was glad she'd remembered that.

"Oh, yeah?" His lip curled up. "Who was it?

"Um . . ." She tried to think. "I don't know his name.

He was medium build, with dark hair. Oh, and he had a scar right above his lip." She lifted her hand from his to touch her lip.

"That's Brian O'Malley. Good guy," he said, sitting back on the couch, seeming to be musing about his firefighter friend. A slight smile kept coming and going from his lips. Then he shook his head as if something had crossed his mind.

"What?" she asked.

"Aw, nothing. Just thinking about the guys at the station."

"What about them?" She smiled, anticipating an amusing story.

"Those guys . . ." He shook his head again. "They sure don't know anything about coffee."

"Coffee?"

"Yeah." He nodded. "Remember when your café first opened? And I used to take coffee to the firehouse?"

She'd actually forgotten all about that until he mentioned it.

"I stopped taking it because they made so many wisecracks about it."

Her face instantly flushed. "Wisecracks? About my coffee?"

Mr. Mulligan waved a hand at her. "Nothing to be concerned about. They just didn't like it—at all," he added, true to his brash style, making her start to feel sick all over again.

"They didn't like it?" she sputtered. "And you never told me?"

"Molly, you don't understand. They're a bunch of

rowdy firefighters. Can't listen to them. They're too rough around the edges, used to drinking any old thing. What would they know about the kind of coffee you make? The same kind my Mary Ellen used to brew. That gourmet stuff. With some real bite to it."

Bite to it? She winced.

"Oh, Mr. Mulligan, the gourmet coffee thing is just a marketing ploy. It's still coffee. And if all those fire-fighters . . ."

Her mind whirled, going a zillion directions at once. How could she have been so blind? How was she going to save her café? And how was she going to spare her elderly friend's feelings in the process?

"Mr. Mulligan, you know what? I'm thinking that maybe those guys at the station don't have the sophisti-cated taste that you do. After all, they weren't blessed enough to live all those years with a wonderful wife like yours," she said, not mentioning the word *coffee* at all. "But, don't you think I should probably consider their feedback? You have to admit, they're a good cross-section of males; a small demographic of coffee drinkers. They sure know more about it than I do. And more than say, April, who doesn't like any hot drinks at all. And—"

Drew. They didn't know more than Drew. Drew who was a coffee drinker and had sampled java from coast to coast. And suddenly she realized—Drew knew it too! And he'd never told her. He said he'd never lie to her or hold back from her. He'd promised on his mother's honor. And yet he'd never said a thing!

She jumped up so abruptly from the couch, poor Mr. Mulligan's head jerked back.

"What are you doing?" He looked shocked.

"I have ten days," she told him. "Ten days left to learn to make coffee and save the café."

"But Drew said I was supposed to watch you. And that you should stay here and—"

"Drew says a lot of things," she cut her friend short.

And then doesn't say a lot of things he should, she inwardly boiled.

"You're either with me or against me on this, Mr. Mulligan," she said, clamping her hands on her hips.

"Ah, geez," Mr. Mulligan groaned up at her, then worked to push himself up off the couch.

Chapter Fifteen

"How's business been so far this morning?" Drew asked Blake after his brother finished ringing up another Corner Coffee Café customer.

"Our cup runneth over," answered Blake, who had been favoring coffee puns the past few days.

Drew looked around the café, and if the number of customers scattered about at the antique oak tables was any indication, business appeared to be even better than the day before.

"I think the banner outside is really drawing them in. I recognize some repeat customers too. I think Molly will be able to pay off Sterling yet." Drew leaned over the counter to high-five his brother. "That's awesome."

"No doubt." Blake smacked Drew's hand. "At one point when Sam and April were both out here helping, we had such a crowd."

"Did I hear my name?" Sam came from the back,

wiping her hands on her bibbed apron. "Do you need help? April and I just put some more muffins and scones in the ovens. Thank goodness, Molly froze all that batter. I hope she's back soon though. Another day or so and we might run out," she informed them. Then smiling up at her husband she added, "I kind of like this job. I think I'll talk to Molly. Maybe I can take more vacation days and spend them working here at the café."

"Spend vacation days here? Instead of on a beach somewhere with Emma and me? Love, I'm afraid that would be grounds for divorce." He glanced at his wife and then Drew. "Get it? *Grounds* for divorce."

Drew and Sam groaned simultaneously. "Trust me, Blake, we got it," Drew told him, as April came from the back to join them.

"Hey, here's the master key for the café." She handed it over to Drew. "Sorry I forgot to give it to you the other day when I had copies made."

"That's okay. I'll try to get back over to Molly's tonight and slip it onto her keychain."

"Think she'll try to come to the café tomorrow?" Sam asked.

"She's doing much better." He nodded. "I doubt if there's any stopping her."

As the impact of his words registered, they all began to look around the café. Sam gnawed on her lip. Blake crossed his arms tightly against his chest. And April fidgeted with her necklace. But Drew knew everyone's body language meant the same thing—they were all feeling nervous about Molly's reaction to the changes that had been made since she'd last been there.

Although Corner Coffee Café didn't look any different, and was just as cozy and charming as always, there were a few new additions. First and most importantly, were the boxes of a tried-and-true coffee to replace Molly's old brand. Next was a machine to make frozen coffee drinks. And the other difference? There were customers, a stream of them all day long.

Could she really, truly be upset about that? Drew wondered. She had called him and Blake miracle workers, after all. Hopefully, she'd still think so when she was well enough to show up at the café.

"Did you make it to the jewelers this morning?" Blake turned their attention to a new topic.

Drew slipped his hand in his pants' pocket, tightening his grasp on the blue velvet ring box there. "Yes. Yes, I did."

"Oh," Sam squealed. "Can we see it?"

Taking the box from his pocket, Drew whispered the prayer that had been his mantra for days now. He prayed that the words he'd heard Molly say were true, that she really loved him. Because he loved her more than anyone or anything he'd ever loved in his life, and he couldn't wait to tell her so.

He handed the box to the women, who oohed and aahed over the engagement ring inside.

"Do you know how you're going to give it to her?" April asked.

"How?" He blinked at her.

"Yes, how." She nodded. "Because the presentation

is very important. Although you are in luck. I read a lot of romance stories, so I have a ton of ideas. Oh, I know." She turned around to the shelves behind her and retrieved a colorful, porcelain teapot.

"This is what you do," she told him matter-of-factly. "When she comes in tomorrow, offer to make her some tea. Only don't put any hot water in the teapot, just the ring. Then when she goes to pour it, she'll hear the clink, open it up, and there it is."

"Hmm . . ." He'd have to think about that one.

"Or you could just slip it onto the spout. Maybe with a pretty ribbon around it?"

To demonstrate, she thrust the teapot into Drew's hands, and took the ring from the box, placing it over the spout.

"That looks pretty too," she said approvingly. "I wish we were going to be here tomorrow for all the excitement," she pouted to Sam.

"Oh, I know. I'd love to see the look on her face," Sam sighed.

"Well, you two ladies might just be in luck," Blake told them both, as he nodded toward the café's front door.

Molly couldn't wait to get to the café and begin researching the art of coffee making all over again. And this time, she planned to perform taste-testing sessions as well.

Due to the busy time of day, she had to park the car about two blocks away from the café. She tried to be patient and walk slowly as Mr. Mulligan hobbled next to her, but it wasn't easy. And now Mr. Mulligan stopped, testing her patience even more. "It looks like people are coming and going out of your place, doesn't it?" He pointed down the block with his cane.

Yes, it looked that way to her too. But that was impossible. After all, she had the key right—

She glanced down at her keychain, fumbling through the keys. No, she didn't have it. But it was always on this key ring. There was no other place it could be. Unless . . . but no, she still had ten more days, didn't she?

"Mr. Mulligan, we have to hurry." She grabbed onto his arm and tried to scurry him along. "Did Drew say anything about Prescott Sterling stopping by my house while I was sick?"

"Sterling, your landlord?" The older man panted. "I don't think so."

"Do you know if Drew gave my café key to anyone? Anyone at all?" She panicked.

"Not that I know of." He shook his head, seeming befuddled by her questions.

But then there it was, when they reached the café, plain as anything. Mr. Mulligan read the banner across the front window. "*Grand Re-Opening.*"

"*Not the same old grind,*" Molly read the next line. "Oh, great. Someone with a dumb sense of humor," she muttered, her ego feeling bruised.

"That's new too, isn't it?" Mr. Mulligan pointed with his cane at a smaller sign on the door. "*Frappu—* what?—*ccinos. Buy One, Get One Free.* I didn't know you sold those kinds of drinks, Molly girl."

"I don't, Mr. Mulligan." She sighed heavily. "I don't."

She had done a lot of hard things in the past few weeks, and pushing open the door of her café—or what used to be her café—was one of the most difficult yet.

Mr. Mulligan trudged in behind her and immediately excused himself to the restroom. And after taking a minute for her eyes to adjust to the indoor light, she stood in the middle of the café, glancing around to check for any changes to her place. None were too apparent except for the addition of the frozen coffee drink machine. And, well, customers sitting at a few of the tables. *That's a change,* she sorely admitted to herself.

Otherwise, the place looked just the way she'd left it. And it broke her heart. Embroidered doilies still adorned the tabletops along with vases of fresh flowers. All the chairs and antique church pews and plaid cushions were still in place. And the ceiling fans turned steadily as if they hadn't missed a beat since she'd been gone.

And that's when it hit her. Having someone else take over her café felt horrible. But having it still look like hers, like the one she'd designed and nurtured, and having it still feel like hers too, was the worst possible torture yet.

As much as she wanted to be in control, it all hurt too much. Her café. Drew. All of it. Tears sprung to her eyes instantly, streaming down her cheeks. Bending her head down, she covered her face with her hands, trying to hide her crying. Shuffling to the side, hoping to get out of everyone's view, she bumped into someone.

"Sorry," she mumbled into her hands.

"No, I'm sorry."

At the sound of the voice, she looked up and couldn't believe her tear-blurred eyes. Drew stood there holding a teapot in his hand, looking somewhat silly, his masculine hand grasping the fragile little thing. But he looked altogether wonderful to her too.

"I really am terribly sorry, Molly. I was simply trying to help out with the café since you've been sicker than the dickens." His voice croaked with sincerity. "But it looks like I've gone and upset you." His eyes pleaded forgiveness.

"You did this?" she sniffled.

"Guilty as charged, I'm afraid. With a little help from my—your—our friends."

Turning his head, he nodded back to Blake, Sam, and April, who she noticed lingering in the doorway that led to the kitchen. The three of them looked unsure whether it was safe to come closer or not.

"But it was all my idea, Molly. So, please, don't be mad at them."

"All your idea?" she asked, wiping tears from each cheek. "How could you, Drew, when I—?"

"I know, I know." He clenched his teeth and his jaw quivered. Then he shook his head, looking totally miserable. "I shouldn't have come in here and made changes without consulting you. Though all I really did was make the coffee better. And I know I should've told you about the coffee before . . . long before. But I couldn't. What can I say? I'm a bloody coward, I am. Too afraid to tell you the truth because I was terribly fearful of the consequences," he said earnestly, his brows creasing.

"No, no." She laid a hand on his arm, looking up into his sweet eyes. "I mean how could you do all of this when I've been so awful, chasing you away the way I did? Drew, I'm so sorry." She tightened her clasp around his forearm, wishing she never had to let go. "You offered to help, and I'm so headstrong and stubborn and—"

"—strong-willed and independent and think you can do everything on your own," he cut in, the beginnings of an amused smile forming on his lips. "And somehow it's okay for you to be there to help other people, but heaven help the person who comes to your aid."

"But I can change, Drew," she interrupted, leaning into him. "I swear I can."

"Change? *Molly Katz, change?*" He looked at her in wide-eyed astonishment. "Molly, I don't want you to change. That's all a part of who you are. And I love you, desperately," he added, his voice so intimate and urgent, she knew it had to be true.

Her heart leaped at his words. "Oh, Drew, you do? Because I love you too."

Once upon a time she would have cared what her customers thought, but times had truly changed. She had missed him so much in the past few weeks . . . had ached for him every minute of every day. She'd missed the sight of him, the feel of him . . . just being with him. And nothing was going to stop her now from crushing herself against him and kissing him passionately.

Except for maybe the teapot wedged in between them.

She backed up from him and rubbed at her rib. "Any reason you're holding onto that teapot?" She arched an eyebrow at him.

"It's for you."

"For me? But it's already mine, isn't it?"

"Actually, yes. Yes, it is. But I, uh," he stammered, "I don't know that you have one of these."

She hadn't noticed the glittering band of silver till he slipped it off from around the spout, and set the teapot down on the table next to them. "This is for you too." He held the ring out to her. "If you'll have it, that is," he added, more shy than she'd ever seen him.

At the sight of the ring, she could feel her eyes shimmering with tears of happiness, sparkling as bright as the diamonds on the ring.

For once she was speechless, as he took her left hand and brought it to his lips. The kiss he placed there shivered a path all the way up to her cheeks. "I've never been one to plan things before. But, Molly, I plan on loving you forever, I swear it. Will you marry me?"

"Oh, Drew! I've never wanted anything so much in my life."

"Anything?" His alluring Dawson smile teased her.

"Anyone!" She held her hand out to him.

Her hand trembled as he placed the ring on her finger. But when he scooped her into the familiar circle of his arms, all felt peacefully right in her world again. His soft lips sought hers, and at first their kiss was gentle, sweet. But then it truly felt as if they'd been apart a hundred years, and, mindless of everyone else around them, they devoured the delicious ecstasy of being together again.

Molly didn't know who started clapping first. It could have been Blake, Sam, April, or one of the customers. She just knew she was glad they were all there to help her and the man she loved celebrate the beginning of their life together.

As the clapping subsided, the two of them made their way behind the counter. Blake reached for her first, hugging her, welcoming her into the Dawson clan. Then, while the two brothers clasped in a bear hug, April and Sam reached for her hand, gushing over the sparkling diamond.

"What does a guy have to do to get a cup of coffee around this place?" The familiar sound of Mr. Mulligan's voice broke through the giddiness. Laying his cane over one of the stools, he worked to hoist himself up onto the one next to it.

"Coming right up," Blake answered him, setting a steaming mug of coffee in front of him in an instant. "Speedy service, eh? One of the *perks* of knowing the owner." He smiled and everyone groaned in unison, including Mr. Mulligan.

"Oh, Mr. Mulligan," Molly sang out. "Look what just happened." She held up her left hand for him to see.

"You're kidding me?" the older man quipped. "You robbed a jewelry store while I was in the restroom?"

"No!" She laughed. "Drew just asked me to marry him."

"Hmm. I'll have to be quicker next time. This time I missed out on the girl. The next time I could miss the entire wedding," he snorted.

"No way that would happen. My wedding day wouldn't be complete without you there to share it."

She came around the counter to give her friend a hug. He flushed from her compliment and affection. "Ah, Molly girl, you know how to make an old man smile." He patted her arm around him. "I'd like to make a toast if that's okay."

She looked up at Drew who had a wry grin on his face. "Do we dare brave another toast?" she asked him, knowing he, too, had to be thinking about the toast his father had made weeks ago.

"I'm game if you are, love." He nodded, and Blake hurriedly poured everyone a small slosh of coffee.

"Mr. Mulligan, the stage is all yours," Molly told him when everyone was set.

The older man nodded and raised his coffee cup. "To Molly, my second favorite gal in the whole wide world, but only because Mary Ellen will always be my first. And to Drew who'd better treat my Molly like she's the one and only girl in the world . . ." He paused while everyone chuckled. "Molly, Drew, as you go down life's winding road together, may you always remember the path to one another's heart is love, gentleness, patience, kindness, respect, and the ability to forgive and forget, and forgive and forget, and—oh, did I say that twice?" Mr. Mulligan's eyes twinkled.

They all laughed before taking sips of the new and

improved coffee. Even she and April managed to down a mouthful.

Conditioned to watch Mr. Mulligan, Molly looked at him, waiting for him to make that funny, contorted face the same way he always did whenever he drank her coffee. But his expression remained unchanged. In fact, he looked rather bewildered, and crooked a finger to draw her closer.

"I'm sorry to say this on such a happy occasion, dear girl, but I think you have a problem here," he whispered.

"A problem?"

"It's the coffee." He shook his head. "What happened to it? It has no bite at all. How are you going to tell your friends without hurting their feelings? Want me to do it?"

"Oh!" She wanted to laugh out loud at this dear, sweet misguided man. "No, I can handle it. But thanks for telling me, Mr. Mulligan. Don't you worry. I'll think of something," she whispered back, hugging him once more.

And she did. Before she even stepped behind the counter to be near her incredibly handsome fiancé, she had thought of a solution—a personalized coffeepot for Mr. Mulligan, for being her most special, most loyal customer. Filled daily, of course, with *her* very own Corner Coffee Café brew. Made just the way he—and only he—liked it.

Epilogue

"**I**s anyone alive in there?" Blake pounded on the door of the alpine condo. "You've been married for more than a month now. You'd think you were still on your honeymoon or something. Hello!" He knocked again. "Drew? Molly? Anyone?"

Drew looked at his beautiful wife standing next to him. They'd finally started getting dressed for the slopes, but it had taken them all morning to do so. They just couldn't help it. They kept getting sidetracked—by one another.

First, they'd cuddled in bed that morning, taking turns telling each other about the dreams they'd had the night before. Then they made their way out to the balcony, shivering but awed by the fresh batch of powdery snow that had fallen through the night.

The snow looked incredibly inviting, but then so did

the hot tub. And it was so close and cozy, right there on the balcony. . . . So more hours, more time slipped by before they knew it. Just like it had the day before, and the days before that.

It had been such a quick week, and Blake was right, they'd barely skied or set foot out the door. Not that they'd meant to hole up from the family, it had just sort of happened that way. But now—now that the week was drawing to an end, they were finally ready to join the rest of the world. And it seemed as if most of the world was there.

True to their word, his parents had organized a Christmas vacation in Vail, renting condos for the entire family. Plus, his and Molly's families had gotten along so well at the wedding that her family decided to join them. Her brother Nick had even brought his girlfriend, a teacher with a broken ankle, who happily watched over Emma while Sam and Blake skied.

"You promised you'd come out on the slopes today," Blake whined again, making Drew chuckle.

"Sounds like he did when we were little tykes," Drew whispered to Molly. "Watch this." He turned toward the condo's door. "We're busy playing Parcheesi," Drew yelled out to his brother.

"Parcheesi!" Blake exclaimed from outside. "What kind of bloody game is Parcheesi, man?"

"It's very intense," Drew answered back. "Very, very intense."

He smiled down at Molly, and suddenly—once more—he couldn't resist the soft lips that smiled back at him. Ski clothes rustled as he moved closer, leaning over to kiss her tenderly, savoring the feel of her lips all over again.

"Oh, yes, right. So intense you can't open the door, eh?" Blake's tone was mildly sarcastic. Then he paused. "If you're playing Parcheesi, then who is winning?"

He tried to trip them up. It worked.

"I am!" Drew and Molly answered simultaneously. Then the two of them broke into a fit of giggles.

"Okay, I get it," Blake called through the door. "But just remember, this is the last day of skiing. Then it's back home. Back to reality," he warned, his voice trailing as the sound of his boots clomped away.

Back to reality.

As Drew gazed at his bride, he couldn't think of a time when those words had sounded better to him. Molly Katz Dawson was his reality, and he couldn't have been more ecstatic about it.

They'd found a home in an older part of Blake and Sam's neighborhood, not too far from Corner Coffee Café. A good thing, since the place was now booming and Molly traipsed back and forth there at all hours. And it was convenient for him and Blake, too; easy for them to get together for business planning.

Plus, often when the four of them got together, they couldn't help but dote on Emma and talk about the future when all their children would play together. Fun-loving cousins, running up and down the tree-lined streets . . . skimming rocks out onto the lake . . . enjoying adventures of their own.

"Two pence for your thoughts," Molly said, zipping up her ski coat, looking knowingly like she always did.

"They're always about you," he told her, holding his ski gloves in one hand, and brushing a hair from her cheek with his other.

"That's one of the things I love about you," she said, thrusting on her ski hat. Her emerald-green eyes sparkled at him. "You always know the right thing to say."

"Hmm. So there are other things you love?" he prodded.

"Oh, just a few . . ." She leaned toward him and kissed him, a glow of warmth spreading through his limbs like the embers of a fire. ". . . a few million," she added, as their lips reluctantly broke away from each other.

Walking toward the covey by the door, he gathered up his skis and Molly grabbed her snowboard from where it leaned against the wall.

"Hey, I'll race you to the bottom of the highest hill out there!" she said in that competitive spirit he loved.

"You will, will you?" He grinned.

"Uh-huh. And I'll probably beat you too," she said smugly.

"You think so?"

"Yep." She tilted her head, and the hair hanging from under her hat fell across her face. She batted her lashes at him knowingly as if he didn't have a chance—in more ways than one. "I know so," she told him.

"What you don't realize, love, is for me it's a win-win situation. There's no losing involved."

Her face scrunched up. "How so?"

"If I beat you to the bottom, I win. And if you beat me, I win too, because I can hang back and watch your incredible body flying down the mountain in front of me."

"Incredible body? You really *do* always say the right thing, don't you?"

"I try."

And he knew he always would try . . . today, tomorrow . . . forever. Because the choice was clear to him. His buddies, freedom, or Molly? Molly was his pick every time.

"So, are you ready?" She placed her pink-tinted goggles over her ski hat.

"Never been more ready in my life," he answered sincerely.

And it was true, he thought, as he closed the door behind them and headed toward the mountain behind his strawberry-blond beauty. He was more than ready to spend the rest of his life loving her, laughing with her, exploring the world's mysteries . . . and counting life's blessings with her.

After all, he realized, there will always be mountains to ski, waves to surf, and so many other kinds of daring feats on earth to try. But in the end, they just didn't compare. Because of Molly, now he knew—love is what it's all about. Love is the greatest adventure of all.